All men are equal until...

by
ANTHONY CLARKE

© Copyright 2004 Anthony Clark. All rights reserved.

No part of this publication may be reproduced, stored in a retrieval system, or transmitted, in any form or by any means, electronic, mechanical, photocopying, recording, or otherwise, without the written prior permission of the author.

Printed in Victoria, Canada

Note for Librarians: a cataloguing record for this book that includes Dewey Classification and US Library of Congress numbers is available from the National Library of Canada. The complete cataloguing record can be obtained from the National Library's online database at:
www.nlc-bnc.ca/amicus/index-e.html
ISBN 1-4120-2012-3

TRAFFORD

This book was published on-demand in cooperation with Trafford Publishing.
On-demand publishing is a unique process and service of making a book available for retail sale to the public taking advantage of on-demand manufacturing and Internet marketing. On-demand publishing includes promotions, retail sales, manufacturing, order fulfilment, accounting and collecting royalties on behalf of the author.

Suite 6E, 2333 Government St., Victoria, B.C. V8T 4P4, CANADA
Phone 250-383-6864   Toll-free 1-888-232-4444 (Canada & US)

Fax 250-383-6804   E-mail sales@trafford.com   Web site www.trafford.com

TRAFFORD PUBLISHING IS A DIVISION OF TRAFFORD HOLDINGS LTD.

Trafford Catalogue #03-2491   www.trafford.com/robots/03-2491.html

10   9   8   7   6   5   4   3   2

Thank you to my family, friends and colleagues who have inspired me to write this love story and also with the design of the cover. Without their help, encouragement and support this novel would have been impossible. It has been a very interesting venture as it allowed me to live in the world of the two lovers when I was writing and left me feeling what they would have felt after wards.

1

Ned was born in late 60's in a very remote village of India. He was born in a big and religious family of ten, five brothers and five sisters. He had a very joyful childhood and was exceptionally ambitious from a very young age and he was known as the daydreamer. None of the brothers and sisters shared any of his personality and character. He used to get very angry when he was questioned about his long and lonely thinking sessions. He attended most of his classes at school but was always unproductive when it came to his exams due to his daydreaming. However, he made it through the primary education successfully although not to his parent's satisfaction. Secondary education was disastrous as he was more interested in galavanting and entertaining women of various age and culture. He never socialised among his own age group and was famous at college. Sporting activities was how he gained his reputation. Ned was always determined to be successful in whatever he did. He went jogging, and attended training with the football, volleyball and basketball team and, mastered table tennis. His interest in studies was so negligible that his father had to change his school to a nearby establishment so that he could be controlled, but that was in vain. He still continued to womanise at school at the risk of being expelled. Somehow he became prominent among his tutors and socialising with them became a norm. His sporting activities brought the college to the light of the media. Through his personal interest, his teachers helped him with his studies. Although he had to repeat classes yet his eminence was tremendous. Outside the house he was the hero everyone wanted to be seen with and at home he was quiet and spent lengthy times daydreaming.

Ned was very energetic and nothing would fail him except for his studies. There were always arguments about his erratic mode of studies, so much so that he had to sit for his 'O' levels three times in order to be successful. Meanwhile at college he had four girlfriends with whom he managed platonic relationships, without being caught even once. Sex was taboo until after marriage but he came close to the experience many times. So close that he was once caught in bed with a girl (by relatives) and he had to run to the fields with his clothes under his arms. Funny! Yes, but not at the time as he was always worried that this unattractive information would get to his parent and that would be a disgrace to the family. So, every time that he was caught he was forgiven due to his disposition of gentleman-like behaviour at home at the cost of being banned to see the girlfriend in question. But as usual there was no difficulty in replacing the ones he lost. "Plenty of fish in the ocean", he used to say. Life carried on inconsiderate of what the consequences were.

2

After secondary education, he decided to give up his studies. It was not his cup tea. Again, with lots or arguments and disappointment his parents allowed him to make his own decision. All the brothers and sisters were well-educated and obtained good results. He was the black sheep of the family. He was then left to his own devices. With no pocket money and no job, Ned had some serious thinking to do. He was faced up with the real world when he went uptown and visited few places for jobs. Nobody gave him a flicker of chance. He went for many interviews with no success. However, in contrast, his friends in similar situations were getting employed very easily, even without interviews. Ned found out that his friends got their job from recommendation and soon it became obvious that it was a case of not what you know but who you know! "Fine", he said to himself. So, there he went looking for political support. To his disappointment he experienced that recommendation was ineffective on its own! It needed to be supported by cash-bribe. Cash he did not have and would not even entertain bribing. He was a man of principles. Therefore, with determination he persevered with his job applications. He collected 150 acknowledgement slips from job applications and 17 refusals of employment following interviews. He soon found out that bribery was the culture and it was suggested that he should consider giving bribe following interviews. This seemed to be the only way to secure a job. Despite tremendous support from the family to find a job and settling down, Ned refused to bribe as this was immoral and against his principles. The whole system was so corrupted that it was unbelievable and disheartening. Hence all these negative experiences resulted in him having a man-to-man chat with his Dad. He avoided arguments, as this would have been seen as disrespectful. This required some courage, oh boy, oh boy! Ned was always sure of one thing, that is, his Dad gave him the 'trust'. Trust was the key factor and Ned braved his way! His Dad was always there for him no matter what the circumstances were. As a result he was reminded the importance of gaining a good education. That was not what Ned was expecting, but still the dialogue was emotional and it was good as they spoke to each other like grown-ups. Life was getting harder and harder to cope with. No money to buy cigarettes anymore. But by magic he used to find a packet of Marlboro lights hidden in his secret drawer (who else could it be but his father).

One morning he got up and said to himself "I am not giving anybody money to buy myself a job. I was born for a purpose and I am going to find my road to destiny".

He went to his father and caught him just before he left for work. He said, "okay ... well I have thought very hard and I want to do something whilst I am looking for a job". His dad said "son, this is very constructive. What can I do for you? You make one step and I will help you with ten. I totally agree that one should not buy a job. I am going to work now and would like to see you at night. Have a plan ready". His dad went to work with a big smile, saying "I am proud of you my son. If you can think this way at the age of 21 then I know you are aiming to be a successful man" and he went to work contented.

Meanwhile Ned went in his room looking for information and replying to job adverts and making his plans towards success. One thing about him was that he always used to write his ideas down and assessed them objectively. A difficult task for a self-starter.

His dad returned from work. Everyone sat at the table for dinner. As usual his dad would feed everyone their first spoonful of food from his plate and then they all ate. It was as usual a cheerful atmosphere with everyone joking and laughing. After dinner, as promised, Ned and Dad met in the lounge and they decided to go for a walk. They went out for a long walk. Ned's dad was an intelligent and understanding person, the best Dad one could have. Ned said, "okay Dad are you ready?". His Dad interrupted, "one minute", and took two cigarettes out of his pocket. Ned was shocked. He was offered the cigarette and he lit his father's and then his. There they walked on the road, feeling at ease and relaxed. It was already half an hour's walk. So Ned started outlining his plan. He said, " I know what I want to do and what I do not want to do". His Dad said, "okay, tell me what you do not want to do first". Ned said that it was against his principles to bribe in order to get a job and he would never do that even if it meant he has to work hard for survival. His father agreed and said, "okay. So what is your hard work plan". Ned said the one idea he had in mind was to grow vegetables and sell in the market and that he would need a small amount of fund and some help with financing. At the same time he would continue applying for jobs and he would start doing some sort of studies that could help him move to other country should the need arise. Ned saw his Dad's face change. He looked surprised, with an expression of sadness, when he heard moving to another country! There was a deep silence with an emotional moment. Ned could see the moment as a flash of lightening which hit his father. After all, it was cultural and traditional in the family to see the children grow and settle down locally as part of the extended family. The typical parents dream in the villages to see the children and grandchildren living close-by until they die.

As always Ned's Dad was understanding and suppressing his sad feelings he courageously said, "son, I will always be here for you in whatever you want to do. All I will ask of you is to take calculated risk. Tomorrow, tell me how much you need to start with the vegetables plantation and how much you will need for the course which you plan to do". Ned already designed his plan and replied, "I have already got the numbers ready… 1000 rupees to start with the seeds and renting a plot of land – one acre, and 500 rupees for the English course. When I recuperate the money through sales, I will return you the sum borrowed". His dad said "when do you want to start?". Ned's reply was "next week". "Next week it is" said Ned's father.

Ned smiled and gave his father a big hug. His dad said, " there is one thing I always want you to remember – no matter what happens, whether you are successful or not in what you want to do, remember I am always here and your family is always here. There is no shame in failure and we always learn and move forward in life. Your home is here for you. If you fail in your venture, there is always other ways. Every time you fall, you get hurt. Remember, look at the wound, and start walking again. Never cry on your wound, it does not help". That was the best advice and support Ned's Dad could have given him. It gave Ned the assurance that he could go ahead no matter what and without pressure to succeed and also he would have the chance to learn by his mistakes. That was Ned's start of learning to live through his experiences and mistakes.

Ned's Dad went home late that night and of course his mother was worried as they were both late. They got in and everyone went to their bedroom as usual greeting each other with kisses on the cheeks and blessings. Ned's mum was very quick in interrogating her husband, as she was always fond of Ned and always protecting him and hiding his wrongdoings. Ned's dad was both sad and pleased at the same time. He said, "tonight I found that I have a son who is righteous in his doings although he is juvenile. I am proud of him. I will help and support him in what he wants to do, even if he decides to leave his motherland." To that Ned's mother started crying and murmured, "what have we not done right that he wants to leave us?". Ned's father did not reply straight away. As a result Ned's father reflected on his past and commented that although he got his job that he well deserved, with regret and in desperation he had to bribe to secure his place. The same applied to his other children because such was the culture within the system of the country. However, if Ned did not want to follow the same trend, so be it and he would respect his principles under no matter what circumstances. Ned's father appeared to be proud when he said, "my son became a man overnight and he is taking responsibilities for his own self. What more can a father expect except to see his children standing on their own feet?". They both shared tears of happiness and went to sleep.

3

The next day Ned got up early in the morning before even his mum and dad woke up. He got his sandwiches ready, had a quick cup of tea and left the house in search of his destination. He walked high and low in various villages, looking for a plot. He eventually found one and sought for the owner. The owner was an old man; sitting in the corner of the street smoking his rolled up cigarette. He approached the man and said, "uncle, my name is Ned. I have been walking around looking for a spot to grow vegetables and happened to come across your land there. Unused it does not look too good, how about renting it to me?". The old man raised his head and looked at him and said, "are you old enough to do this?". Ned said, "age has nothing to do with this, rent it with me or shall I seek somewhere else?". The old man said, "I would rather earn the money than someone else". They agreed the sum to be paid for one year and it was promised to be settled when Ned started using the land. It was a big plot of land to manage single-handed but he was determined to do it for himself. Following his encounter, he went home. He walked all the way to save the bus fare and reached home just in time for dinner, all sweaty and out of breath. He dropped his bag on the floor and sat next to his mum as always. None of the brothers and sisters had the slightest idea as to what was going on. Everyone was talking and eating. For everyone it was a normal day and business as usual. Ned's dad was as usual listening to everyone and treating Ned like everyday, as if there was nothing special although one could see the esteemed look for Ned in his father's eyes. His mum was quiet and pretended that she knew nothing. She was sad and she was offering Ned everything she could see on the table as if to say "you are trying and I am here". Her eyes were full of tears but she controlled them from rolling out. Everyone finished their dinner and they all retired in their room. Ned caught his dad on the way and told him about the land he had negotiated. His dad was pleased. And they all went to their bedrooms. Ned was awake in his bed and planning. He wrote down; 1. plantation, 2. studies, 3. leave, 4. where, 5. how, 6. when. He put his paper in his folder and went to sleep.

Next morning he woke up late, as he was very tired. He sat on his bed and said to himself, "that's my life and only I can get on with it". He dragged himself in the kitchen, without noticing his mum he went and made himself tea. His mum came from behind and touched his shoulders and said, "are you tired? Do you want me to make breakfast for you?". Ned replied, "it is okay, I will have to learn to do it myself. I cannot expect you to do everything for me?". Ned's mum was touched and said, "well you are still my baby just like the others". So they sat down and talked about various things including the plans that he had discussed with his father. And he also mentioned that if nothing worked out then he would try other countries. His mum tried to keep calm to this discussion and said that she wished him to be successful at home with her around. However, if he had to leave home and country then she wanted him to know that although she would miss him, she would support him and always love him no matter what and where. Ned's said, "well do not black mail me. It will make it harder for me if ever the time comes". Ned's mother replied, "in my one hand there are five fingers, cut one finger out, does the others function the same way? Do they all not hurt?". Ned remained quiet for a moment and reassured his mother that no matter where he would be in the world, he would always make sure he would keep in touch on a regular basis, but again he did not know if he was going anywhere. They were quite satisfied with the conversation and Ned went to his room and got ready to go out. He had his breakfast that his mum made whilst he was getting ready and started walking. This time he knew exactly where he was going. He walked to the college and walked in the principal's office. Of course he was well remembered there. He was greeted like the hero. He was offered tea and he talked to his principal about the possibility of taking a private sitting for an advanced English course. He outlined his studies plans to his principal. He would do his learning at home in his own time and sit for the exam, in this way he would only pay for his exam fees, thus reducing the expenses. Due to his reputation and to the satisfaction of the principal, it was agreed. He was registered on the same day. He bought his books and walked back home.

Ned went straight to his room and started planning his schedule for studies and his work. As usual he wrote his plan and this time he stuck it to the wall. His plan was to get up early in the morning at 5.00 am and start studies, finish at 7 am then have breakfast, prepare lunch and leave house to go to the field at 8 am, come back from the field at 3 pm and spend time with his mum and dad with household chores. In the evening after dinner he would go to socialise with his friends and be back by 10.00 pm. After that he would study until midnight. Quite a tight schedule to follow on a daily basis but he was determined to achieve his ambitions. He finished planning then he came downstairs for dinner. He then went straight to his bedroom. His dad went to see him before bed to get an update. As promised the funds to get Ned started was ready in time. So Ned started his routine. Early Monday morning he got up, studied, had breakfast and got ready for work. He wore his old, broken trousers and shirt, took his hoe on his shoulders and off he went. He walked all the way to the field. On the way, he came across his friends who were on their way to work well dressed. To his surprise none of them acknowledged him on the road as if he was non-existent. It was a typical attitude of the society with class status and looking down on poorer people. He thought "that's life... who needs friends like that?". He reached the field, had half an hour's rest and started clearing the overgrown bushy field. The sun was burning in the sky. He looked up and acknowledged the heat and then continued to toil. All alone in the field, his patience was infinite. By lunchtime it was so hot his feet were cooking in his boots. He took them off during lunch, had half an hour's rest and continued with all courage until 3 pm. He stuck to his target. He finished on time, looked at how much he had done and smiled. One acre is quite big, but nevertheless it was his work. He calculated that it would take him about two weeks to clear everything and get the land ready to sow the seeds.

He picked his tools and walked back home. On the way he met the same people. He waved at them and this time he did not wait for responses. He continued with pride. His girlfriends were soon to be ex-girlfriends as he was not the same clean man they knew at college. He reached home about 4 pm, had his shower and carried on as planned. In the evening he went to meet his friends at the café bar they used to spend their time together. All of them were there. He went to join them at the table. One by one they all disappeared to other tables with different excuses. It was not difficult to assume the reasons for their behaviour. He continued with his drinks, and left at 9.30 pm. He walked alone in the dark night with his hands in the pockets as usual, singing along as if nothing happened. He was a great character and nothing would upset him. He knew what he wanted from life and he was going to get it regardless of what anyone would think of it. He got back home and went for his studies. He was burning the midnight oil without thinking. He was so engrossed in what he was doing that he lost track of time. This was his first day and nothing would stop him. His dad could see the reflection of his light from his bedroom. He secretly peeped in to see if he was okay. Ned was busy with his books and papers. His dad went to the kitchen discreetly and made him hot milk. He took the drink to his room and asked him to drink it and helped him to bed. Ned asked him to wake him on time in the morning. He fell asleep in seconds.

His dad woke him up on time. Ned got ready and stuck to his routine. Day in, day out he persevered for two weeks. His land was ready and his studies were going well. In his venture, there was his dad, his mum, and him. His brothers and sisters were always busy. They used to meet only for dinner where they used to share the events of the day. Ned was always quiet at this time because his events were not interesting. Instead he chose to lead the prayers before and after the meals. He made it a habit to help his mother with the dishes in the evening and tidy the house. Ned chose the most unpopular route towards starting his honest life and his parents were really proud of him. His social life disappeared within two weeks, as there was nothing to go for. Instead, he used the two hours to read various types of book. His favourite was the encyclopaedia 'understanding human behaviour'. He used to read ten pages before his scheduled study time and used to get into deep thinking mode. He used to write a lot; plans upon plans. His room was full of note pads scattered everywhere. He would not let anyone read them and would not allow anyone to throw them. They were all his brainteasers.

Ned was on target with his plantation schedule. However, he had difficulty in deciding as to which vegetable would be profitable to grow during the season. This was where he needed his mum's and dad's experience and knowledge. He went to the market everyday for one week and looked for the availability of different vegetables whilst preparing the field. He met with his mum and dad in the evening and they decided to grow three different vegetables with the possibility of covering any losses due to seasonal mass production of the same vegetable. They finally decided that they would grow tomatoes, long chillies and aubergines to start with. Also, they advised Ned to grow coriander in the interim because these herbs are fast growing and can be profitable with early crops. For increased profitability he was advised to trade and sell his own produce. That was agreed. Next day, Ned took money from his dad and set off to the city and bought the seeds. He came back home with three heavy bags. By the time he came it was time for dinner and everyone was there. The brothers and sisters became curious and inquisitive about Ned's adventure. He took this opportunity to explain. Unfortunately, whilst the venture was not met with disapproval, there was no forward coming support or offer of any help. His father listened quietly and said absolutely nothing. His mother said that she would help if he needed it; still no one offered his or her help. They all agreed that it was hard work and this was not an understatement as Ned already knew it from the previous two weeks, as he has been in the field everyday.

Next morning, after studying Ned set off to the field. On the way he met the old man, the proprietor, and they both walked to the field sharing their experiences of working as a labourer. The man looked at his land and he was shocked and astounded to see the great job Ned had done. The old man was so delighted and encouraged that he stayed with Ned and helped with the sowing of the seeds. They chatted away sharing their experiences and stayed in the field until dark. Ned's father was worried, so he came to see Ned in the field. There, he saw Ned and the old man just about finishing the day's work and packing their tools. Ned's father was impressed and they walked back talking about their day. The old man told Ned's father that he had a diamond in his house and that he was precious. He said he could feel success coming his way and blessed Ned for a bright future.

Ned and his father got back home. Ned was tired. His father made him a cup of tea and served him dinner. And it was the best thing his father could do to encourage his son. They sat together eating their meals whilst Ned's mother watched over them. Following his hard day Ned went for his shower and looked at himself in the mirror. He looked darker and rough with cuts and bruises. His eyes were sunken and he felt tired. He could not recognise himself. He looked at his hand and it was all getting hard and rough and full of cuts. He looked at himself in the mirror with his eyes full of tears. He said to himself, "I am only just 21 years of age". He murmurs, "right, I need to revise my plan. I have to think of overseas. I am still young and full of energy. And I have no money but I have style". He smiled back to himself and rubbed his fingers through his hair. His whole thinking was changing. He was smiling all the time. He got out of the bathroom completely refreshed. New ideas were roaming in his head. He met his mum on the way and gave her a long hug. He went to his bedroom turned the lights off and went to sleep.

Around 2.00 in the morning Ned jumped out of his bed, got his book started studying. He studied until 7 am. There was nothing much to do in the field except to watch out for the birds and the growing plants. So he took his books, pen and papers to the field with him. He was there sitting on his own, thinking. After a long while he took his pen and paper and started planning. At the top of his page he wrote "vegetables", at the bottom of the page he wrote "England". Next page, he wrote, "what in England?". He was thinking!

He walked around in the field looking at his work and admiring what he had achieved in three weeks. He came back to his papers. He started writing and developing his ideas. Money, he wrote down, between vegetables and England. That was his first part of planning. He started counting how much it would cost to go to England, United Kingdom, with fares and hotels for three months. He would need approximately four thousand pounds until he stabilised himself and started settling down. But how was he to get the money and also return the funds he borrowed from his dad. His plan was such that he would sell enough and make at least 6000 pounds to cover all costs and have some left over for any emergencies.

Next day, before going to the field, he went to the library and looked for information about England. He brought all information with him to the field. He read line by line and thought hard. His attention was suddenly drawn to an advert to join nursing education in London or anywhere in the UK. He did not waste time. He wrote a letter requesting information and an application form. On the way back home he posted it.

He ensured nobody knew about it at home otherwise he knew it would start his mother crying. He continued with his routine of field, and studies everyday. Every now and then his father would visit him in the field to see how his crops were doing. He was pleased to see the coriander growing fast. He could also see the tomato, chilly and aubergine plants growing. They were both proud and delighted. Smiles were beaming on their faces. Everyday for the following two weeks he started pulling out the coriander plants, which were ready for sale. His target was two hundred kilos daily until the field was empty. One acre of land with coriander was quite a handful. His dad noticed that he needed some help. Ned would not ask anyone but every afternoon his dad came to help him in the field voluntarily. He brought his harvest at home in big piles which he carried on his head all the way from the field. His mother helped with quality control and tied the corianders into various size bunches ready for sale. Although Ned did not ask for any help, no offers were forthcoming from any brothers and sisters. They looked at all the tedious messy tasks and one by one they soon disappeared to their bedrooms. So, after having a rest Ned and his father joined in sorting the coriander. After they had their meal with everyone at the table they continued with the task at hand. The daily chat at mealtime was decreasing gradually. Ned was busy. After his meal he would get in the middle of the coriander and start working. It took an entire month until they finished with one acre of harvest. Ned stuck to his studies. After getting everything ready for the market for the next day he would get cracking with his studies. He would sleep for two hours and get ready for the market in the early hours of the morning. He had to wait for the truck at 2.00 in the morning to take him to the city. From 2.00 in the morning in the lorry, they would stop at various places to pick others until the lorry was well overloaded. They finally reached the city's market at 6 am. They had to be very quick to set the tables and their vegetables, as the public would start rushing in at 7.00 in the morning. Having been up from early hours, by the time it was 7.00 in the morning the sun was already rising higher. Ned could not look up in the sky because of the strong and the bright glow. It was getting hot by the minute and that was not good for fresh corianders. He had to sell quickly before he would not sell anything at all. Ned was bright. He always brought his sunglasses with him. He wore it and looked like a young, modern, and attractive salesman. He would easily attract young and old women to his table for sale. From 7 until 9 he met his target. Everything sold; he counted his income daily and was doing quite well. Following each sale Ned would separate his income into, money for his father, money for his mother, money for his personal expenses and money for England. He would return home by bus and go to the field after lunch and continue. This went on for a very long month. Everyday he looked at himself in the mirror and talked to himself. The only line one could hear was, "I can make it. Nothing is going to stop me now". He was quite melodious with his returns from his first sale and that was more than enough to pay his father back. He did not tell anyone anything and kept all money locked in his cupboard. He did not dare tell anyone just in case the next harvest would not be as productive. He was quite tuneful. He was going to the field everyday and the next harvest would be tomatoes. That would be harder than the first one. Picking tomatoes one by one from the big field would take endless time. So he was working extra hard at his studies. The following month he approached his principal and suggested to sit for the June exam which was in two weeks. His principal agreed as he could see Ned's determination in his eyes. He wished him all the best. Ned went home, studied hard at home and in the middle of working in the field where he had his books. Meanwhile in the field his father was coming everyday to help him irrigate the plants and helped him spray the nutrients. It was not easy work. His father would carry water in small drum on his head all the way from the main water fountain, getting wet with the water overflowing while he was walking. It was a sight for memories. They did not give up. That was done twice weekly so that the produce would be excellent. They persevered. They took turns to fetch water and sprayed the solutions for healthy growth. They got home exhausted at night. Ned made sure he gave his dad a good massage before he went to bed so that in the morning he would be fit for work. Ned's dad never moaned because he was helping his son to get out of this corrupted world and he was protecting his principles. As a loving father he was fulfilling his duty. His mother would look at him with pride. Everyday she gave the other children their lunch box in their bag and all properly done and presented. They were all neatly dressed before they left home for work. Whereas she found more pleasure putting Ned's lunch in his old, dirty and ragged bag, and waving goodbye for the field was always emotional. Tear of happiness would roll off her eyes. She would look at him walking down the road until he was not visible. She would get back to her housework afterwards.

One day Ned returned from work and found a letter on his table. The letter was not opened or damaged in any way. He gave a sigh of relief. He went straight to his mother and asked when she received it. His mother could not read or write so he was safe and his secret plan was safe. He hid his envelope in the drawer and went downstairs and pretended as if it was just another application form. But he knew this one was a totally different type of application form. Ned continued with his usual routine. Late at night after his homework, he carefully filled the application form and got it ready for posting in the morning. He went to bed that night. All he had in his mind was money, England, nursing, new life, and a new beginning. He wanted this to happen for him so much, his heart was set on it. He worked hard in his field and all he had in his mind was success. Without a successful harvest nothing would be possible.

His harvest came one after another. He became well-known in his little village and at the market in the city. It was only six months since he started and got quite famous. He was determined and he had a good sense of humour. He would not allow any comments to upset him. He was focussed and very quickly he saved the sum of money he needed. The tomatoes were harvested and the season completed. Chillies crop were to follow and these were harvested when they were in demand at an expensive season. The harvest would be profitable. He looked tired and worn out but he would not give up. His routine was important for him. Meanwhile his exam results came and he was so delighted that he passed. He jumped up and down with happiness. His brothers and sisters could not believe it. This was Ned who took more that one sitting for the most wanted exam and this exam in English was the most important of all and he did it in three months. What an achievement! He was the talk of the village. From a person nobody wanted to know in the village suddenly became an idol! Everyone wanted to be his friend. Ned never refused anyone his hands for friendship but the one lesson he learnt from his previous experiences that friends would always remain friends; blood was thicker than water and would always be. His popularity increased his sales. He did not miss an opportunity to miss an opportunity. He used all his avenues to make a good profit. His mum and dad were proud of him indeed, and his brothers and sisters too. After another few months, Ned received another letter from England. This time his dad received it as he was home. It was very unusual. He took the letter and kept it in his room until Ned arrived home at night, of course his mother did not have a hint of what was happening. Ned's dad was a highly reliable person and would not mix issues with others who had nothing to do with it. He could notice the letter was from a school of nursing. His mood changed as he could feel that he was going to lose his son to another country. Somehow he accepted it before Ned came back home. He called Ned to his room and they had a long chat in the light shade of the room before he gave him the letter. Ned told his dad his plan with all honesty. Then his dad gave him his letter and said, "I assume you will be leaving us soon". Ned was shocked and did not know what to say. He tore the envelope open with the speed of light. "I have been offered an unconditional seat at the school of nursing" he said with excitement. He was in tears, then his mother walked in. She saw him crying, she started crying without knowing the reason, then his dad said, "Ned will be going to England soon". To that, his mother started sobbing non-stop. This encounter woke everyone in the house. Ned shared the news and they celebrated with a drink in the middle of the night. Ned made a request to everyone that absolutely nobody should know until he has bought his ticket and got his visa in his hand. That was agreed and they all went to bed.

The following morning Ned woke up and he made his way to his field and also posted his confirmation of acceptance for his nursing course on the way. He worked hard in the field. He seemed to have endless energy. His dream was coming true and he needed his last push. To his astonishment he saw his brothers and sisters walking towards him in the afternoon. They all came to help him and gave him a last minute boost so that he would meet his target. They came to assist him every afternoon until his crop was finished. Meanwhile Ned bought his ticket and got his immigration papers ready. As it was a small village, the news travelled fast from the travel agent to the villagers that Ned was leaving for London. In his last week, everyone would stop him for advice and with hundred of questions as to how he managed it all by himself. Ned's reply was, " I made one step to help myself and the rest came from above". He was never rude to anyone, and of course he was very thankful to his dad for his help and support.

The day before leaving Ned went to the city for some last minute shopping. On the way he stopped by a famous palm reader. He was always interested in palmistry and had read many books in this science. He wanted to give it a try. He went in and had a reading for twenty rupees. The palm reader said to Ned, "you will be successful in whatever you do. One thing you never do is show your palm to anyone when you are in London". Ned was shocked. "How do you know I am off to London?, he asked. I can see it in your palm but the truth is that I can see your ticket through your shirt pocket". The palm reader folded Ned's hand starting from his finger and rolled it into a fist. "Keep this hand locked for you only" he said. All the best and remember your roots. They said goodbye and never saw each other again.

Ned came home with bagsful of shopping to take with him. One would think nothing was available in England. He took everything to his room and got himself packed. On the eve, they all had a special dinner and they invited few friends and families. They had a dinner and dance party. It was great. Everyone was drunk except Ned and his father. Ned was staring at the sky and thinking about the next day. His father was looking at him as if he was taking a good stock for his eyes. His mum was in tears all the time but satisfied that his son made it at a young age. Of course his friends and ex-girlfriends came to say good-bye. Without failure all of them asked Ned to set them up in UK after he has settled down himself. Of course Ned's reply was, "yes, definitely". In his mind he knew exactly what he had to do.

After the party was over, all the guests went to their own home. The house was quiet again. They were all sitting in the lounge. So, Ned requested everyone to stay there while he went to fetch something from his room. He came back with a box. Everyone was anxious to know what was in the box. He pulled out his plan and tore it and put it in the bin. Next he took out a paper which contained the account for all his investment and expenses. He gave a packet of cash to his dad and thanked him for the loan. He took another pack of cash and gave it to his mum for personal expenses. He gave his brothers and sisters small presents and a token each. He took out another pack of cash and said, "this is for me to settle down in UK until I start my course". He took out another pack of cash and gave to his dad to clear all his debts. They were all shocked. It was unbelievable. All in less than a year? They all shared tears of happiness and sorrows. Ned's determination gave everyone a lesson and he told his dad, "thank you for everything, and mostly thank you for buying me life and not a job". They were all proud. That night Ned looked at himself in the mirror and said to himself, "world, now its you and me!". They all went to bed. Ned's father came to him at night, before retiring, and said thank you to Ned for showing them the way and wished for more youngsters like him who would go forward in life without shame and shyness, and without fear. Ned went to sleep but kept waking up every now and then. Excitement, anxiety, worries; this was the longest night for him.

Ned got up early in the morning although the flight was not until the evening. He went for prayers early, came back home and started his last minute packing. The day was going too fast. The last day at home appeared very short. Everyone was busy doing nothing. There were lots of last minute visitors coming all the time. Ned's mother was busy entertaining them and everyone one of them was blessing Ned. It was a very busy house.

At 5 in the afternoon, Ned took out his luggage and brought them down. At this time Ned's mother broke down in tears, she could not help it, it was real, and she came out of her dream. She always thought he would change his mind at the last minute, but Ned was more ready than ever before. It was a moment of emotions. Seeing their mother crying, all sisters joined in with their tears. However, they had to send Ned off with good wishes and some prayers. Ned's mother brought her prayer book, recited few verses, gave him a kiss and asked Ned to close his eyes and sit down. Ned did as asked. He sat down. His mother took off his shoes and socks and wiped both soles of his feet with new and damp white handkerchief. Ned kept his eyes closed, as he was not supposed to see the handkerchief until it was out of sight. His mother put his shoes back on and took the handkerchief in Ned's room. It was supposed to be an old tradition where you leave all bad luck behind and take a fresh step to life with fresh feet. When his mother came back he opened his eyes, she put a sweet in his mouth and said good-bye and asked him not to look back once he was in the bus. Ned's mother and father stayed at home whilst all the brothers and sisters got in the minibus they hired for the occasion. They all got in. Ned was in the front passenger seat. His father came to him and kissed him on the cheeks and said "play your cards right and do not forget the ace in your sleeves". No tears and no fears, Ned waved good-bye. Once the bus moved he did not look back as instructed by his mother.

Behind him, his mother and father were sharing their tears. They could not help it but at the same time they knew that he did it all by himself only. They were proud of him. They both went in the house and prayed for his success in whatever he was going to do. Meanwhile, in the bus there was an air of silence, the real thing was happening, they were going to lose their brother. After all they have never been apart for a single day in their life. Ned's sight was fixed on the windscreen. The others were looking sad. After a long journey, they reached the airport. They helped Ned to unload. They all went with him to the Check-in desk to assist him. Ned did not want to see anyone crying, so he suggested that they go home before it was too late and they all shared hugs and kisses. Needless to say the tears were flowing like there was no tomorrow. Ned showed no signs of emotion. He was numb and he wanted it over and done with. He asked them to look after their parents and that he would keep in touch with them on a regular basis.

Ned went to the departure lounge and sat down. He could not believe that it was all happening. He missed his family very much but at the same time he knew that he was doing it for a reason and for himself. He was tired and fell asleep on the chair. He was in a deep sleep and dreaming about his landing in Heathrow. His mind was so busy he did not hear the call for boarding the plane. The information department was calling his name and he still did not hear it. He was fast asleep, recovering from his hard work. One lady sitting next to him happened to see his name tag on his hand luggage and gave him a nudge, and said, "young man it looks like that you are in the process of missing your flight. The last call for you was about 2 minutes ago". To that Ned jumped, he put his hand luggage on his shoulder and started running. He never ran so fast in his life. He zoomed through the double doors and corridors. They were just about closing the doors when they saw him coming, puffing along. They opened the door and welcome him. He was out of breath and sweating, and of course with all the strong curries he had the night before they could all smell garlic all along the path! The airhostesses showed him his seat and helped him settle down. It was complicated for Ned as this was his first flight, but it all went okay. He sat down and greeted the passenger next to him. She was white and English. As known from his earlier days, he was not shy with girls and so he settled down in a pretty long interesting conversation about schools days. They were talking and laughing all the way. The girl, Joanne seemed interested in the conversation. They shared jokes and talked about sex! Ned was quick with this line of conversation. Little did Joanne know that Ned was still a virgin. He had lots of girlfriend but he was still celibate. Yet he could hold the conversation in such a way as if he was an expert. The Indian lady behind them could not resist listening to their dialogue and every now and then would give a cough so that Ned would get the warning. But not for Ned, he gave the lady a dirty look and continued. That was an enjoyable trip for him. First English girl and he was there, in his element. They enjoyed their meals and fell asleep. Ned started dreaming about England again, this time he woke himself up as he dreamed that the plane landed and took off again whilst he was sleeping. He jumped and woke Joanne, he shouted, "are we there yet?". Joanne replied, "no, not yet. Do not worry, I am going there as well". He went to sleep until the plane started descending. At this point Joanne wanted Ned's details. As Ned was new in the country, she offered her telephone number and offered her assistance should he need it. They walked all the way towards the immigration officers where she left him and waved good-bye. He said to himself' "another good bye, when are the 'hello's' coming". He queued in the never-ending long line. He was tired with the journey and just about standing in the long queue. Everyone looked so worried and gloomy in the queue. However, after an hour's long queue he finally came to the immigration officer who said, "hello, good morning and welcome to London". Ned was surprised with the tone of dialogue and welcome and said, "if the officers in high places in my country were as good as you then I would never have left my country". The officer smiled and said "Thank you, Sir. May I have your passport and the purpose of your visit please". Ned thought "Sir! I must be very important". He straightened himself and lifted his droopy shoulders and handed over his passport and nursing letter to the officer.

He read the nursing course letter and looked at Ned with a Gay-ish smile. Ned looked at him and felt uncomfortable. He wanted to run, so he took few steps back. The officer stamped his passport and said, "it is this way, Sir", with a gay-ish tone of voice. Ned turned around and then turned around again and reversed in the opposite direction. He never came across gay man before and he was embarrassed. He turned around again and covered his back with his hand and his hand luggage. It was not enough; he was running and falling at the same time. It was a laugh. And nobody could understand his behaviour. He felt better when he was out of sight. He went to collect his luggage and got out on the street.

The expression on his face was good for a picture. He looked up, looked around; all he could see was white people. He smiled and said to one of the passers-by, "I have seen you in James Bond". The passer-by looked at him and said "get real". "I am Ned, and I am real", Ned replied to the gentleman in a polite manner. The man walked off. Of course in the middle of nowhere, Ned looked at the instruction sent by the college of nursing and made his way to the nurse's accommodation by underground train. He was looking around in amazement and his head turned around in all direction. He was in another world.

4

The train stopped at his station, Ned was surprised that people who he would classify as strangers were helping him with his luggage. He started liking the culture and the generosity of the people from the first day. He caught the bus with the help of the local people and headed to the hospital. Once there, he located the admissions office where new students were being received and welcomed. He went in, introduced himself, and his particulars were thoroughly checked. They were all gathered in one big hall and the principal lecturer delivered his welcome speech. Following the speech, all students acknowledged each other, and talked about where they came from. Basically they socialised whilst the accommodation officer was allocating each individual with his/her room. In the mean time Ned was happily looking at the exquisite, good looking and pretty girls. They all left home for the first time and were engaging themselves in nursing. Ned looked around and counted 10 men out of 60 students, him being the only male foreigner. Therefore his chances were quiet good, he thought. He liked his girls. It was not long until few girls wanted to know him. So, everyone exchanged room numbers so that they would meet in the social club at night. After they received all details about starting college they all left the hall. He went to his room with his luggage, opened his door and looked around, and murmured "one single bed, one table and chair for studying, one shelf, a chest of drawers, a cupboard and a sink... will have to do". "Good start", he said to himself. He dropped his bags in the middle of the room and lay down in bed. He thought of his parents and brothers and sisters. He missed them very much. "What are they doing now?", and straightaway he found the nearest phone box and called his mum. Ned was close to his mum and he was never away from her before. "Hello mum, its me, I am here". His mum replied "I hope you are well? Have you had dinner?". Ned did not want her to worry so he said "yes, I did" and he told her about the meeting with the students. It was a quick call. Ned was conscious and was careful with his expenses. He went back to his room and sat on bed and he could feel the whole world falling apart. He started thinking whether he made the right decision and he started doubting himself. He loved his mum and everyone very much and he missed them. He started reviewing his entire decision. He walked around and thinking that he had everything back home and yet felt as if he had nothing. In contrast he thought "well, here I have nothing but I can have everything in the future", and it would all be his own doing. He felt himself filling with energy and determination. He felt lifted and got his little stereo out of his luggage and put the music very loud. He started dancing and dancing until he was wet with sweat. The other students upstairs could not bear the loud music and came to his door. They were banging the door but Ned was so far gone that he could not hear a thing. The girls pushed the door open and could see him dancing all wet with sweat. They went to him and held him to stop. He was embarrassed and stopped and turned the music down. He apologised. It was quite funny as the girls liked the way he danced. They introduced themselves again and planned to meet at night for a drink. Ned was embarrassed and could not refuse. The girls left his room with a smile as if they were going to a competition and the question was, "who was going to get this catch?".

Ned unpacked and settled down in his room. After a short rest, he went for a shower only to find out that there was a bathtub. He never had a bath before, only showers. He was not used to this style of living. However, he had to get accustomed to it. He filled his bath, got his bar of soap he brought from home and his scrubber. He was finding it difficult to cope with it as he kept slipping and sliding down in the bath. The idea of soaking himself in the bath with his underwear on was not very appealing to him. After struggling to keep his balance he managed to scrub himself clean. He was disgusted to see the colour of the bath and with the soap he used there was a thick black rim on the edges of the bathtub. He was not sure of it. After draining the water he started to scrub it clean. He managed to do it. It took him longer to clean than having a bath. By the time he got back to his room it was already 8 in the evening. He got ready in his best outfit, applied his cosmetics and his best aftershave. He was just about ready when his new-found friends came to collect him to go to the social club. The girls were impressed as he looked really cool and they all walked to the club that was 2 minutes walk from the student nurses' accommodation.

They walked in the small club and filled it with students. They were welcomed with a complimentary drink. They all sat down and the atmosphere was buzzing. The social club members were friendly people as they were all employees of the hospital and they all had been through similar experiences. They were all mingling and getting to know the people in their vicinity. For the old members of the club it was the time they could pick their partners for the next three years and they were all trying to chat the girls up and trying to invite them for a drink in their rooms or inviting them for parties. Everyone was talking to someone of the opposite sex. The drinks were flowing. The jukebox had a busy time with the latest dance tunes. Needless to say that those who were already drunk were swinging with their newly found temporary partner, may be one-night stand, or may be few days or weeks relationships. It was all happening in that small but lively place. Ned was in his entertaining mood and was chatting to few of the students he met. But his main aim for the evening was to observe and learn about his new environment and the behaviours of those in it. He had his drinks and was merry. He was being chatted up by the girls and accepted invites for drinks in their rooms. He was not aware that in accepting the invitation meant he would be spending the night. Therefore he said yes to all the invites and he felt famous and was blissful. By 11.30 at night the social was closing and everyone was going their way. As Ned accepted few invites the girls were waiting for him to leave. When he stood up, four of them stood up with him. He walked to the door with a trail of women behind him. He stopped and said, "okay lets have the drinks". The girls looked bewildered and they could not understand him. Ned went to his room and they followed him! And he was now confused and did not know what to do. He opened the door and went to lie down on his bed. All the girls jumped on him. He went in a panic and was fighting back. It was a sight for a video recording. They were all drunk and were trying to undress him. One had his trousers, one had his shirt, one had his vest, and the last one had his shoes and socks. Ned woke up from his drunkenness and merry self and found himself running away in the corridors. Running away in his underwear and the wild women running after him woke everyone in the nurse's accommodation. They were all calling out, "hey stud, save one for me!". It was funny, first time in a strange country, first night, and first experience with women; Ned found it difficult to cope with. When the chase stopped, he apologised to the girls and went to bed. Of course the girls had a good laugh and there was no hard feelings. They all retired to their corners.

Next morning he got up early with the alarm clock ringing in his ears. It was the first day for college. Ned got ready in a flash with a soaring headache. He went to the canteen for breakfast and met the other students. Of course the previous night was not forgotten. He was welcomed, "good morning stud!" he heard. He looked around and found few of the students having a giggle. He did not mind. He joined them with his breakfast and they all shared the first night's experience away from home. They all walked to the meeting point where the coach would pick them up. College was about an hour's drive, so Ned fell asleep like many of the other students. He woke up when they were all getting off the coach. They were welcomed by the tutors and guided to the main lecture hall where there were about 110 students. They were all fresh for their first day. They had a welcome speech and the tutor also made a joke about someone being chased in his underwear in his first night in the nurse's accommodation. Ned was surprised how fast news travelled up the hierarchy. But it was a good laugh and the tutor said he wished that the entire course would be as fun as their first night. To that Ned felt quite comfortable, as it was nothing to worry about. The tutors shared their experience of living as a student nurse and they were quite similar stories. One warning though, "be careful with your milk, this is one commodity that disappears quickly from the kitchen fridge", the tutor said. To that there was a big laughter, and Ned could not work out the funny aspect of the comment. Anyhow, he thought, "oh well, let's laugh". After all he had to pretend that he was conversant with the ways of thinking.

The first day was full of information giving and sharing and everyone had to introduce himself/herself in front of the whole group. Ned was shocked with the calibre of students; it appeared to him that he was the only student who had the lowest qualification to join in. A lot of them were degree holders, attended private schooling in UK and most of them had completed 'A' levels. Nevertheless, Ned went to introduce himself. His speech was simple, "I am Ned, I am not as good as any of you, but one thing I know is that I want to be a nurse, I want to be a successful nurse and want to have as much fun as I can to complement this academic journey. I believe there is no tomorrow, and I want to make the most of today and everyday, as a student nurse. ... and... ". To that everyone started laughing. "Of course outside being a student" Ned continued. That was the end of his introductory speech! There was no mention about his personal life and where he had been educated, or about his qualification. Of course the tutors knew about his background through his application form, yet they were impressed about the way he managed the introduction. One of the tutor said, "unusual but impressive". "Thank you, Sir" said Ned.

On the first day, they were familiarised about the college and the facilities available. Ned was impressed with all the facilities students can have as well as studying, libraries, gym, swimming pool, football, volleyball pitch, table tennis, squash and all. He was well in his element as he was very sporty. The first day, at lunch in the canteen, there were small groups forming already. Ned's group had only women and himself. That could be identified clearly and there was already a sense of jealousy as being a foreigner he already had attracted many women and everyone was commenting about him and his first night, and his jovial introduction. Most of the girls were in competition in getting him. But Ned as usual liked the company, as he did not show any interest in any of his companions as yet. He did not believe in asking women to come to him. He was waiting for everyone to find their partner and he would look for the best among those who were left behind. His idea and rationale was that, those who look fast are desperate, emotionally unstable and would be trouble. Hence, he waited. He continued to have a lot attention. He was observing, having his lunch and enjoying the show. Ned was different; he had his own ideas, and his own philosophies.

College started well. The next day, it was full-blown lectures and seminars. Little did anyone know that Ned was not used to these styles of studies. The language was a problem. His spoken English was good but not good enough for high-level education. During the first lecture he felt nauseous and sick, as he could not understand most of what the lecturer was talking about. The spoken English was different and the vocabularies were beyond his understanding. He ran out of the lecture theatre, rushed to the toilet and was vomiting. It was his nerves. He was in tears as well as being sick. He could not stop. Whilst he was in the toilet he had to sort his mind out. He started thinking of his purpose in England and reviewing his decision. He had to do it no matter what; for himself more than anything and not for anyone else. After clearing his head, he went back to the lecture theatre and apologised for the disruption and joined the session as if nothing happened.

Ned started writing down all the words he could not understand instead of taking notes. He knew he would pick up the lecture's content from the books. His lists got very long by the afternoon. After college he looked at all the words in the dictionary and started familiarising himself with them. He took his oxford dictionary and terminology dictionary with him. On his lunch breaks he would look up the word and got better quick. He was able to directly understand the lectures without having to look at dictionaries. He was three weeks in the course and was making good progress.

He used to go to the club every night after his studies. He used to return home after college, have a cup tea, listen to the radio for about half an hour to clear his head, then have a bath and review his daily lecture notes. He would then do his reading for the next day and then go to the social club for a drink. He went to the club late at 10.30 in the evening. The reason for doing so was to spend enough time to socialise with the others and secondly have enough time just for one drink. He had to stick to his budget. The plan was working out well.

5

The fourth week at college, there was an announcement. There was a new student joining the course late. Her name was Mary. Mary introduced herself and came to sit, luckily next to Ned. She was from a very religious family from Shannon in southern Ireland. She was an observant catholic. She was about five feet five inches tall and pretty with blue eyes. After the session Ned and Mary got chatting. She told Ned about her background and her families. She came to London on her own with no friends and family. As it happened she was staying in the same nurses accommodation as Ned but in a different block. After college, on the way back, they sat together in the coach. They spent a long time knowing each other. Everyone was envious of Ned. They were attracted to each other form the beginning. Once they got off the coach, Ned offered to show Mary around and planned to meet her in the club in the evening.

Ned went to his room and rushed with his routine. Although he met this pretty girl, he did not forget his purpose and his goals in life. As planned he met Mary in her room and they shared their experience of living away from home. Mary was a degree holder and already experienced what Ned was beginning to know. They had a cup to tea and set off for a long walk to the shops and went to accustom themselves with the bus routes and the facilities around the area. They got back around 11.00 in the evening and went straight to the social club. As soon as Ned walked in there were cheers to welcome him. Mary was quite surprised to know how popular Ned was in the club. Of course it was not long until she was told about his naked chase. Mary was not impressed as she already started to like Ned. After one drink she went back to her room on her own. She ignored Ned for the rest of the evening. Ned acknowledged her disappointment but did not miss having a good time in the club. As usual he would not let anything ruin his moods and upset him. To him, it was like, 'either you like me the way I am or lump it'. He would not change for anyone and kept his identity. After the club, Ned went back to his room and continued with his studies. He went to sleep around 2.00 in the morning. Meanwhile, Mary was hoping that Ned would visit her after the club, and kept waiting until she could not hear anyone walking back from the club. Afterwards she kept peeping at Ned's room and saw the light was on until late. She thought that Ned would come for a visit after all but little did she know that Ned was committed to his works. She waited until Ned's lights went off. Mary went to sleep even later than Ned.

Next morning, Ned complied with his usual routine. He met Mary in the canteen. He was ignored. Mary talked to everyone except Ned. Ned was not bothered. To him it was business as usual. He did not even assume that Mary was waiting for him after the club. He was having his breakfast as usual and chatting to everyone else. Of course he liked Mary but would not make it obvious. After his breakfast, he walked to the coach with the others with Mary still ignoring him. In the coach Mary sat on her own, and Ned was reading his book. At college Mary ignored Ned.

In the afternoon class the assignment topics were distributed by the tutors. Ned was not accustomed to the writing style expected in England. It was the first 3000 words assignment in his life. He was only used to writing a maximum of 600 words essays. That was difficult for Ned. In the classroom he asked questions about writing style and was not very welcomed by other students. Therefore he gathered that 3000 words was a normal length for an assignment. The session finished, Ned ran out of the classroom and went to the toilet where he was vomiting. He felt sick, as he could not work out how to do it and felt ashamed to ask anyone. The thought of writing an assignment caused him to vomit. One student saw him in action at such an unpleasant time and had to call a tutor to help him. The tutor came and inquired about Ned's health. Obviously Ned was fine but he could not put himself down and did not tell the tutor the real reason for his nausea and vomiting. The tutor provided Ned with a carrier bag and drove him to his residence. In the car Ned could not help but vomit. It was a disaster. All he could think of was his failure and his future. Once at the nurse's residence Ned got out of the car and pulled himself together and dragged himself to his room. His tutor accompanied him up to his door and ensured he was safe and then left. In his room Ned was in tears. He did not know what to do and how to do. He started thinking of a way out.

Meanwhile, after college, when Mary did not see him in the coach she got worried. Not only Mary but also everyone was concerned about Ned whereabouts. As soon as Mary returned, she went to see Ned first. She knocked at the door; there was no reply as Ned was in deep thoughts. She pushed the door and got in after knocking several times. When she looked at Ned, he was still in a dream-mode. She went and sat next to him. To that point Ned was startled and panicked. "I am sorry, I did not hear you" he said. Mary did not mind and asked Ned, "what's up?". Ned said he did not know, he just felt a bit down and needed sometime alone, so the tutor gave him a lift back. Mary did not believe him and pushed and tried to explore more of Ned's behaviour. Mary continued to ask Ned for the truth as she said she was rather concerned that he was not well. Ned got annoyed, as he did not tolerate pushy people. When he said he wanted to be alone, he meant it and he kindly said to Mary, "please Mary, I need my own space for few hours. Please do not push for an explanation. I will talk to you when I am ready". To that Mary commented, "is it to do with last night that you want to shut me out?. Ned could not bear the inquisitive nature and the blackmailing style of Mary. So, he lost control and shouted back, "just leave me alone. I said I will speak to you about it when I am ready. I think I was quite clear in my language. So, please go and if you want I will pop in to see you later, if it is okay of course!". Mary did not like being shouted at and replied, "suit yourself!". She stood up and rushed out slamming the door behind her. This reaction of Mary annoyed Ned very much as he was never a rude character. He only wanted some peace and quiet and some time to think about his difficulties. Of course for Ned it was a big problem as that was his top priority. Ned helped himself with a cup of tea and remained in bed till late. Afterwards he went for a long bath. He then thought that if he told Mary perhaps she would help him with some advice and practical help. After all she was the only person who cared for him at the time. So he thought about Mary and later felt better. He planned his conversation to Mary, withholding personal details about his personal life and home life as much as possible. At the same time he had made his own plan about his learning process and how to go about writing a 3000 word essay without anyone's help just in case Mary would reject him. He got out of the bath, and started his daily routine late. That evening he did not go to the club. Instead he looked for information that would help him in his works. He felt better and more positive about doing the assignment. It was difficult in the beginning but then he started writing, writing anything he could extract from the books and anything that came to his mind. His whole point was to write and gather as many ideas and relevant points as possible to devise a frame for his assignment. He got so engrossed in his studies that he lost track of time. Meanwhile Mary was waiting for him in her room. Ned did not forget about Mary, he was looking at the clock every few minutes, as he really wanted to see her, but had to give enough time to his main priority so that when he went there he would not feel guilty. Meanwhile Mary was getting impatient and annoyed with Ned. "Who does he think he is? How can he treat me like this?", She kept repeating to herself.

She waited until 2.00 in the morning. Ned's reading light was still on. So she decided that she would go to see him and confront him. She got out of her room, banged the door behind her and marched to Ned's room. Without knocking the door she pushed herself in. As soon as Ned turned around to see who was there, Mary apologised. "I am really sorry, I did not realise you were busy with your studies. I thought you went to the club and came back without seeing me,.." Mary shamefully exclaimed. To that Ned stood up and in an instant reaction, he grabbed hold of Mary by her waist and gave a deep long kiss. He was shocked and so was Mary. They both started apologising to each other. They sat quietly in bed. There was a long five minutes silence. Mary was a religious Catholic girl and Ned, a womanising dreamer. "Just what was happening?", Ned asked himself.

The silence broke when Mary asked Ned, "so, are you ready to talk?". Ned smiled and said "yes, now I am". "I do not like your sarcasm", murmured Mary. "Honestly, I am ready. So what did you want to ask me, Mary?", asked Ned. So Mary asked Ned what the problem was and Ned gently explained Mary about his worries. Mary listened but did not offer to help. She just listened. As Mary did not offer, Ned asked if she would help him with the structure of an assignment. Mary was caught in, she liked Ned and they just kissed, and she enjoyed kissing Ned, she could not say anything but yes. Ned gathered that she was unwilling but there was no one else to ask for assistance. Mary reassured Ned that he would be fine and that he would survive. Whilst talking to Ned she looked at all the pages Ned had written in the first day of receiving the assignment criteria. She felt quite envious and jealous. She thought, "he cannot find a method or a way and yet unknowingly he already knew the best approach or method to apply!". She stared at the papers and then sat on Ned's bed. She knew already that Ned was not only handsome but also had academic capability and potential.

They sat on the bed together. Ned was a hot-blooded character and Mary was a redheaded Irish girl. Both knew what they wanted but could not make the first step. Ned was embarrassed as this was his first time alone with a white girl. He did not know what to expect. Obviously the scene was different from a movie where the hero just threw the hot woman on the bed and started kissing. Then he thought he would make the first move. He gently grabbed Mary's hand and said "let me read your palm". Although Ned could read palm through his knowledge of palmistry, yet this time it was not to read but to hold Mary's tender and soft hands. Mary was not innocent either because she knew exactly what was in Ned's mind. She handed over her palms to Ned and said "I hope you can really see what is in there!". Ned took her hands and said, "you are a very intelligent person, very strong and level-minded. You are conscious of who you are. You will be married and will have four children. You will finish your Nursing course with flying colours". After that Ned stopped. He closed his eyes and started stroking Mary's hands and arms. Mary did not resist and was enjoying it. Gently they started stroking each other, from the arms to the shoulders, the hair, and they reached each other below the waist. Ned was in his element. He was enjoying every moment in this first encounter. Mary had both eyes closed and was enjoying Ned's magical touch. They were in a totally different world. They started kissing each other in the lips. It became wild, and they were both hot with desire. Ned was impatient as well and he undressed himself down to his underwear. Mary was in another world and did not realise that Ned was naked. Ned slowly and gently started to undress her. Ned took her t-shirt off, then her trousers, followed by her bra. She was still enjoying her experience. Ned got to the knickers when Mary stopped and sat up in bed. "I am sorry I did not mean to lead you to it" she said. Ned said "that's fine. If you do not want to go ahead it is ok" although he wanted to go all the way. "I am still a virgin", said Mary. "That makes two of us" said Ned. Mary did not believe Ned. She got her clothing and said "I do not like liars". Ned did not bother explaining. Mary left the room with Ned still looking at her with envy and desire. Ned got up after cooling himself down and got to his books. He was aware that he was alone in his studies and continued gathering his information for the assignment. Mary went to her room and was surprised that Ned was still awake after 4.00 in the morning. Ned was very stressed. He then reflected on the past and remembered the hot blazing sun and the struggle to plough the plantation field. He worked without rest then and so this current stress made him more determined to work harder still. He thought to himself, "it is to make it or break it". He became more productive. He did not sleep that night. At 7.00 in the morning he went for breakfast and walked to the coach with Mary as if nothing had happened. He was not upset with Mary's behaviour or comment. Mary apologised for her behaviour for the previous night.

They sat together in the coach and were holding hands. Ned was confused, but then he did not want to make an issue of it. He played Mary's game, whatever the game was.

They had a normal day at college. Ned went to the library at lunch only to find that there were no books in the subject area in which he was going to write his assignment. At that moment getting the first assignment right was a major aspect of his course. He went to the librarian and requested information about where to get the books. He had to buy them and that was guaranteed. He worked out his budget quickly in his mind and ordered two books that were going to be delivered in two weeks. Whilst he was ordering the books from the bookshops area of the library, Mary walked in and of course she saw what Ned was up to. She made no comments and they walked back to the coach to get back home.

As soon as Ned got off the bus he went to his room and started with his routine. He went to the club late and came back to his studies as he planned. In the club everyone was asking each other how they were getting on with their home works. Ned did not say much to minimise any embarrassment. One week went by with Ned trying to cope with his studies. He felt like swimming in the middle of the ocean with no direction, totally lost. The only positive thing he did was writing continuously so that he would not feel as if he was doing nothing to help himself. He always believed that, "god helps those who help themselves", therefore he was doing his best. As time went by Mary knew Ned's study and social routine. She chose to visit Ned when he would come back from the club every night. Ned was polite and would welcome Mary whenever she came to his room and most of the time it would be when he was attempting to study. Every time Mary would come to Ned's room, she would ask how he was getting on, and Ned being honest, would give her all the details. When Ned asked Mary how she was getting on with her assignment, her answer was standard, "I have not started with it yet, cannot decide what topic to choose". Ned believed it and he shared his books that he bought with her. She declined Ned's plea with a witty excuse every time. Every night since they first kissed, Mary visited, they lied down in bed and cuddled for long time and every night it was the same old story, "sorry, I am not ready for it yet". Ned never made an issue of it as he was easy going. The routine for Ned was becoming demanding. He would not go to sleep until he had completed his second session of studies after Mary left. It was becoming tiring. He was lacking sleep. He looked tired and worn out. He could not work out what was happening to him, it could not be Mary because he enjoyed her company, and she enjoyed visiting him at night. Mary on the other hand looked fresh and in high spirits at college, and very lively and chatty.

One day Ned came back home after college, earlier than usual. He decided to have one afternoon's break. He slept until 10 in the evening to catch-up with his sleep. He went to the club and met with his friends. There he met someone called Shah and they found out that they were from the same country. They chatted for a long time and caught each other up with the latest development. After a long chat with Shah, Ned explained to him about the situation with Mary and his tiredness. Shah had been in UK for 10 years and knew exactly what was happening to Ned. He, in few line told Ned, "I know about your problem already and many people in the club know about it too. It is the person you are going out with, she is taking the 'micky', and she is using you and making fun of you with others. That's the truth, now it is up to you. Remember, if you need me I am in the same block as you, third floor. My name is on the door". They finished the subject they were talking about. It was 11.30 in the night. Ned was sitting in the club, and thinking. He was finding it difficult to believe that he was already receiving advice from someone he briefly met for approximately 30 minutes. However, Shah appeared to be genuine enough. There again, Ned decided to find out for himself.

He left the club at midnight. He went to his room and put the light on and left the room immediately. He did not know what to think and what to believe. As he never had a chance to visit Mary in her room he decided to take a stroll to visit her. Unknowing to Ned, Mary had already checked if Ned's light was on which indicated that he was in his room. Ned went to Mary's door and stood there quietly and he was thinking whether he should go in or not and of course Mary was not expecting him. After a discussion between him and he, Ned knocked at the door. Mary's calm and sweet voice replied, "come in". She did not look up to see who was in as she thought it was one of her female friends. Ned said, "hello Mary, sorry if I am disturbing you but I thought I would pay you a surprise visit". Mary was sitting in the middle of a pile of papers and books. So she quickly shut the books, and gathered all papers and stacked them on the desk. "I am trying to work out what to do, it is so difficult and impossible, it is unbelievable" she said to Ned. Then when she finished tidying everything, she invited Ned to sit down. While she was packing everything up, Ned recognised his books and similar books from the library. He said nothing, and sat on the bed. It was a decent room, effectively decorated and had everything that showed Mary's interest. He noticed things that Mary never talked about. "I am very thirsty" said Ned. Mary offered Ned a cold drink but Ned wanted an exceptional cup of tea. Mary went to the kitchen to make the tea. Meanwhile Ned became suspicious and curious to find out what Mary was up to! He opened Mary's files and flicked through them. He found that Mary's assignment had all ideas similar to his and interestingly enough the title was the same too. The assignment was nearly completed and she was tidying up the reference list. He was shocked. He put everything as he found them and lied down on the bed pretending to have fallen asleep. After about five minutes Mary returned to the room with tea. She sat next to Ned and as usual started the same old conversation and moaned about how difficult it was and she did not know what to do. Ned made no comment. He felt hurt and deceived. He felt at a lost and hard to hold his emotions back and prevent tears. He felt betrayed and used by the only person he trusted at the debut in U.K. Ned thought to himself that he knew he was notorious and playful but he was trustworthy; honest and faithful too. He had personality of an extrovert and was open and helpful to anyone close to him. It was his first experience of being let down. He was disappointed with himself for allowing him to trust someone. He was blaming himself and not Mary. She was only trying to survive and survival it was for her. He had his tea. He did not even touch Mary and was leaving the room. Mary stopped him for a kiss. Ned remembered the words from Shakespeare's Julius Caesar "Et tu brute". Then he kissed her good night and went to his room.

Ned had to decide what to do next. But this time he was too hurt to do anything, he felt used and abused. He blamed it on his innocence and gentlemen-like behaviour. He went to sleep. In the morning he got up and stuck to his routine and the usual day with Mary. He was quiet all day. When he went to the club he met Shah and told him what happened. Shah explained to Ned how an assignment must be structured and written. He was grateful for this advice that he had been searching for so long, and he got it from someone he hardly knew. Shah and him became the best of friends from then onwards. He came back home that evening after the club and started to do his works. He changed all his works, from title to main argument. At 1.00 in the morning, he locked his door and turned the lights out. He went to sleep. Mary came at 2.00 in the morning and knocked at the door. She even tried to push the door open. Ned heard it and was tempted to open the door and let her in but he resisted. It was hard for him. She was his only comfort. He listened to the continuous knocks and kept quiet. He did not open the door. He said absolutely nothing. He went to sleep, and slept well. He felt a lot better next morning. He went to college, sat away from Mary and continued his routine as usual. He chatted with

Mary but nothing meaningful. At home that night he did the same as the night before. And this went on for three days altogether. Mary asked Ned several times if there was anything wrong with him and his relationship with her. Ned never replied to her questions. Of course everyone knew although Ned did not say a word to anyone. Mary also spread rumours that Ned was gay and that he was having personal problems and that he was having difficulty keeping a relationship with her and that he was confused. Ned never replied to anyone about these comments. He concentrated on his assignment. He did it and got an 80% marks. Mary looked at the published results and she could not believe it. She made an appointment with her tutor and asked how it was possible that she had the same assignment and she got lower results. The teacher was shocked and asked Mary how she knew it was the same assignment. Mary told her half the story and she was humiliated when the tutor explained that Ned's assignment was totally different to hers. Mary was ashamed and since then she was always in competition with Ned. Mary and Ned kept in touch but only as classmates and nothing more. Ned was deeply affected by Mary's betrayal and deviousness. It was a lesson that would be never forgotten.

Although he missed an opportunity to enjoy himself, he would not allow his burning desire to success to be dampened or hindered by Mary's behaviour. He put it down to a learning experience. Mary never knew why Ned distanced himself from her. In fact a week after separating from Ned, she met Brian and she slept with him on the first night. Ned was not upset about it. In fact it made him suspicious and careful of women. Mary was some virgin indeed! Ned thought, cheap enough for a one-night stand. Ned was glad to know that he had a lucky escape. Rumours spread that Mary claimed she was depressed because of Ned. And again no one paid attention to her, as they knew how she used people. She ended up with no permanent boyfriends and became known and the 'bike'. Ned maintained contact with her as an acquaintance and nothing more.

6

Recovering from his first unpleasant experience about women, he soon learnt that most women in the club culture were the same, that is, out for fun. Ned had to get accustomed to it. He started going to many parties at the club and became very famous for his hip gyrating, sexy, and provocative dance. He would never be on the dance floor without more that one woman. He was always dancing with more than one and sometimes it would end up in fights. It was good, as well as studying hard and burning the midnight oil, he was having the best time of his life. He was invited for private parties every night. He would go to them but always sleep in his own bed, all by himself. Regardless of his happy-go-lucky nature, he was not a one-night stand person. He had certain morality and self-discipline. He used to get drunk on party nights without failure. Ned's attraction to women was unexplained. The fellow members of the club, students and nurses were all envious of him, his women chatting-up abilities and his dancing. He was always there. He was always triumphant and successful.

The days went by, he was well in tune with his course works and was achieving above 80% in all his assignments. He also achieved outstanding marks for his hospital placements. He used to walk in wards and the whole atmosphere would change. The patients were happier. "It was so admirable to receive care with a compassionate smile" they would say. Many commented, "do you 'tippex' your teeth every morning". It was great. He came from an average background and was doing well in England, not only in education but also socially and in his chosen career. He had many women friends but no girlfriends. He was not bothered, as he was a virgin. He did not know the taste of sex, and what he did not know, he did not miss. To him it was normal. The first year at college went by. He had two months for summer holidays. He could not be in London and do nothing.

Therefore Shah and Ned planned a camping trip to the Lake District. Neither of them had travelled that far in England before, and they decided to brave it. After all, Shah had a lot of annual leave days and the nurse's home was nearly empty as most of the students went home for summer holiday. Shah rented a Nissan Micra and Ned made provisions for food. They piled the small car with their duvets, pillows, bed sheets and clothing. They also took with them a traveller's gas cooker, small and useful. It was great and they were both excited. They checked the weather forecast in the morning. It was supposed to be sunny with the temperature at 27 degrees centigrade. The weather would be stable for the whole week and that was a bonus. On the way to the motorway they bought a map. Ned planned the route whilst Shah drove. They drove along and every two hours they had a break. The services on the motorway were too expensive for

Ned, so they had their sandwiches and crisps in the car. On the way they chatted and shared their experiences. Shah and Ned became very close. Shah was the only person Ned off-loaded to and they continued. Shah had been in UK and was in Ned's situation, so he knew that Ned needed support. Shah could see that Ned was a genuine person and hard working so he offered to help him in any way possible whenever and wherever needed. From 8.00 in the morning, they reached Windermere at 5.00 in the afternoon as they were driving slowly and carefully. They drove around and located a campsite. They drove through the gate and paid the fees for five nights in the campsite. They drove through the many tents and settled in the far end of the site so that they could be discreet as it was their first experience. They looked around and looked at all those tents. The others were all professional campers and had all the necessary gears and items and the latest big tents that one could walk inside without having to bend down, kneel or crawl. Shah and Ned looked at each other and started unpacking. They had to read the manual in order to fix the two-men triangular tent. They could not get it right. It was blowing everywhere; they kept getting wrapped up in it. It was a good laugh. Two of them were making more noise that all the campers together. They knew they would have a good time. It took them two hours to fit the tent and get all settled in. By the time they finished there was no time to cook anything special. Shah was tired from driving and could not keep his eyes open. So Ned quickly boiled some water and made some noodles. It was simple but effective. They got under their duvet and fell asleep quickly.

In the middle of the night, Ned woke up with a funny noise. It was a loud squeak, and was getting louder and sharper. He was getting scared, as he believed in ghosts. He did not want to disturb Shah and was trying to find comfort in Shah's snoring. After trying for few seconds, he could not relax and he could not sleep. He was sweating in the mountains of Lake District. He finally decided to give Shah a nudge. He woke Shah up after few nudges and kicks on his legs. Shah woke up quite concerned. Ned told him what was happening and Shah found the noise quite unusual as well. He was experienced and had been around for few years but this sound beat them all. They were trying to compare the noise. They squeaked and thought it was an owl, squeaked again, and might be a bat. Every time they imitated the sound they got a reply. Every time the squeak was getting louder and louder! They were both getting worried. Ghosts, may be!. They had to be brave and see what it was otherwise their entire camping trip would be spoiled. So they both zipped out of the tent, walking behind each other. Just ten metres away from them there was another tent. The noise was coming from inside. The nearer they went, the louder the noise was getting. It was strange. They were discreet, and thought they would open to see just in case someone needed help. They bent down and knelt on the wet grass. Ned pulled the zip down and closed his eyes tight just in case it was something horrible while Shah watched. The zip went down, Shah saw what no one should have seen, and what couples do in private at home. They were a young couple having the best time of their life in the tent. The woman who was on top felt the cold wind on her back and looked back and screamed. To that Ned opened his eyes and froze for few seconds, meanwhile, Shah was running as fast as he could. When the man sat up in the tent and stared at Ned watching his naked partner, Ned got out of his dream and started running. With the woman's scream, everyone was out of his or her tent looking at what was happening. They were laughing at Ned and Shah being chased by the naked couple. They were not difficult in being identified as they were noticed when they were putting up their tent. It was not difficult for the naked couple to locate Shah and Ned either. After few minutes, Ned and Shah had visitors. They both apologised and explained what the situation was. They were all laughing and had few beers together afterwards. They were lucky they were not beaten up. They all got drunk and they retired to their own tents. Ned told Shah, "I will never forget what noise people can make when they are having fun, good night". "Good night" replied Shah and they fell asleep. The next morning when they got up their noisy neighbours were not there, but the grass underneath the tent was dead with the heat.

They prepared breakfast erratically as they were both not so domesticated. However, they made it despite taking longer than usual and planned their day. As they were camping on a hill they thought they would climb the peak. They packed their sandwiches and set off. On their way they came across many people who were from the same campsite. They were remembered from the previous night and they were acknowledged. The campers were friendly people and it was no offence. Shah and Ned were the only foreigners in that area and climbing. Everyone had their climbing and walking boots with the right outfit while Shah and Ned had their usual jeans and shoes. When they got remarks about their gear they said "we are techno-climbers". They were warned of the slippery surfaces. Shah and Ned did not worry about it as they were used to such climbs. They were fit and they climbed very fast. They ate their sandwiches and had their drinks while climbing. Other climbers were surprised at the speed they were moving. They reached the top in half the time and took pictures. They admired the view and sat there for about half an hour, quiet and breathing the fresh air. It was wonderful. Nothing could steal that moment from them. They did not talk at all during that time.

After few minutes the weather showed signs of changes. "That's English weather for you man, can never trust the weather man!" Shah said to Ned. They started to climb down. They could see the rain coming towards them, but it was too late. They were going to get wet anyway. They were soaking and enjoying the cold rain and running down without slipping. The other walkers and climbers were shocked by them. They definitely had good control of their feet, as the ground was slippery. They ran down all the way to the campsite. They definitely had a good time. It was 2.00 in the afternoon, still very early but nothing much to do with the rain pouring. They went to the showers, enjoyed the hot spray and made a mess everywhere. They came out all refreshed and got in their tent. From 3.00 in the afternoon until 7.00 in the evening they played cards and drank wine. They made more noodles and continued with their games evening. Outside they could hear people coming back from their outings. Some were complaining about the weather and some were even talking about going back. Shah and Ned already paid the whole amount for their stay so, come whatever may they were staying. After all it was an adventure, 'one enjoys the good with the bad' and it was more fun when it was an unusual one.

Shah and Ned were having an out of the ordinary evening with playing cards in the wet and windy weather. About 9.00 in the evening, they ran out of wine and all they had was hot water in the thermos flask. They had to keep themselves warm. The layers of T-shirts, shirts, and jumper and leather jacket were not enough for Windermere. They had lemsip to start with so that they would not catch flu. After lemsip they could not go to wash the cups as the facilities were quite far from their tent. So they had to continue with lemsip-flavoured tea, then tea flavoured coffee and then coffee flavoured coke. It was amusing for them as they never had such experiences before and had they not had an unusual holiday they would not have known what unusual tastes of those combination would have been. They amused themselves with the various flavours. Half way through the night they needed more drinks and there were no hot water. The weather was only getting worse by the hour. They did not want to risk boiling the water in the small place they had, which was full of duvet covers, bed sheets and their usual clothing. They needed to get their hot drinks sorted out. They had to decide what to do. They were sitting down in their two-men tent trying to work out what to do. "We might need to go out and boil the water in someone else's tent or ask someone to give us some water" Ned exclaimed. Shah was not thrilled with the idea, "over my dead body, I would rather stay as I am until the morning" Shah replied. But then he was getting cold and the weather was not helping. They decided to use the public facilities to make their tea. It was not an easy decision as they had already ridiculed themselves with the people around them but again it was late at night therefore they wanted to risk it. Both of them got ready, took their equipments and ran out. They reached the place where they thought they could boil the water but it was too windy and the rain was reaching inside. They both looked at each other and went in the toilets. They cleaned one of the cubicles and were boiling their water when one of the adventurers came to use the convenience. He heard two men talking in the toilet in foreign language and straight away he knew who they were. He started shouting at them and throwing some really disgusting comments. Ned and Shah were frightened and did not know what to do. They remained quiet and suddenly the man burst the door open to disturb their peace and quiet. What he saw was quite the opposite of what he thought. He apologised to them. They got talking and of course the man shared their tea and took some hot water for his family as well. He said, "only foreigners have these natural survival ideas while we sit in our tent waiting for some miracles". Ned and Shah felt complimented. At least they were not disgraced for their action in the toilet. They were finishing up when they saw other men coming with their equipments to do the same. It became a rather social two hours in the toilet in the middle of the night in the middle of nowhere amongst people they did not know. Quite an experience!

They went to their tent afterwards only to find out that it was flooded. Unfortunately, Ned did not zip up properly. There they were, everything was soaking wet. What next! They got in the car for the rest of the night. They continued with their game of cards and their variety of drinks with a variety of flavours. They were having a good time despite their misfortune. They finally went to sleep at about 5.00 in the morning.

They woke to the heat of the sun. The weather was nothing like the night before, very hot and sunny. They looked where they were sleeping, the car was muddy inside and they were wet as well as their tents. Whatever they laid their hands on were wet and smelt unpleasant. They looked at the tent; it was flat on the ground. They got out, stretched themselves, made their tea outside and went to have a wash. There, they met the people they shared the toilets with on the previous night. They had a cheer and they got engaged in the night's experience. The campers offered them help with their tent and belongings but Shah and Ned refused, as they did not want to get embarrassed. They got back and packed everything in their car except for the tent and drove to the nearest laundrette. In the laundrette they found that everyone had similar problems and all the washing machines were engaged. While they were waiting they had hot drinks. When they got a machine, they took everything they needed washing out from their black bin bag. To that, all the campers turned their head towards them. One of them asked, "have you camped before?". Ned said, "no, but we are techno-campers. We have not got the right gear but we, surely, are having a good time". They all started laughing and making fun of them. Ned and Shah did not pay any attention to them. The man who boiled water with then in the toilet the night before came to their rescue, "hey lads, you might be fully equipped and experienced with these type of adventure, but you surely do not know how to have a good time. We are from the same campsite and believe me I have never had such an experience camping until I met these two young lads, especially when you need boiled water in horrible weather. So mind your business and leave them alone!". The man turned to Ned and Shah and gave a nudge of approval. They felt great after that and carried on with their washing.

After completing their washing they came back to the campsite and rebuilt their tent. This time they chose to be near the fence to be safe (just in case) from the strong wind or bad weather. Luckily the weather was good from that day onwards. They enjoyed sunshine and late nights. They even went to an Indian restaurant one evening. The owner of the restaurant was so overjoyed to see his countrymen that they got a massive 50% discount with their meal. It was excellent. They shared their camping experience with the owner of the restaurant and enjoyed the time. The next day they went to visit Keswick, a noticeable, old town. They felt like they travelled through time. They enjoyed learning about the culture and met some friendly people. Everywhere they went they were greeted with respect and dignity. People were different compared to other places. Ned started to like English people and the culture. Shah and Ned had a good time since then. As their shoes were wet they put on their socks, then a Tesco carrier bag then their shoes. That protected their feet from getting wet. They left Windermere after their stay was completed. They made many friends and exchanged addresses to keep in touch. On their way back they stopped at Blackpool for the evening. They spent some time in the casinos and amusements. They spent a little fortune playing the various machines, mostly 2 pence and 10 pence machines. They had fish and chips on the beach late at night. They were approached by many women who wanted some company but they declined and they were even branded gays. They did not pay any attention to any comments and they enjoyed the peaceful time on the beach. They stayed up all night and left Blackpool at 6.00 in the morning for the nurse's home. On their way back they stopped at the services and had tea and lunch. It was rather expensive but they thought they would enjoy luxury for a change. They had their oriental songs blaring in the car and they drove back slowly and safely to the nurse's accommodation. They were home, sweet home. They were tired but full of energy. They settled down and afterwards they washed the car inside and out and returned it. Shah went to his room and Ned retired to his room for a short rest.

As both were addicted to the social club, they could not wait to go back and have a drink and meet the rest of their friends. At 9.00 in the evening, Shah came down to Ned's room and they both went to the club. In there, they talked about their experience and had a good laugh with the others. The night went quick and they were both drunk. They went to their own room and they were not seen by anybody until lunchtime the next day. They certainly needed a good sleep in their soft and warm bed, a big difference from sleeping on the ground. The days went by, Shah and Ned met in the club every night. Ned kept his study routine religiously strict.

7

Came September, the new intake of student nurses were announced through posters stuck on the wall in the club. The date and time were already decided and the college was looking for volunteers from second year student nurses to welcome the new comers. Ned knew that it was his chance to get to know new people and he knew that all males were waiting for their opportunity to get their catch! Little did he know that he changed and he was among them too. He did not miss an opportunity to miss an opportunity, so he volunteered. He was well known at college and the tutors could not find anyone better than Ned to start the new students off. The date and time of new students were noted and planned. He opted to receive them himself so that he would know everyone and their particulars (room numbers!). On the day he was given a room that he used as a little office where he welcomed each and every one of them, one at a time. He had a name list and the room numbers. Ned could not be any happier as there were many who would have liked to have those details. He kept himself very professional and he promised not to give anyone those details no matter how friendly the person was, and that included Shah. He was going to keep the task he was entrusted with, and he did. One by one the students started pouring in the room. They were many, some coming alone, some with parents, some with friends and some with brothers and sisters. Ned welcomed them, showed them the direction to their rooms and asked them to meet him in the club for an introductory get together. Out of all girls he found one that he fancied. He did not know why but he felt attracted by her. She was English and cultured. She came with her parents, respectable people and softly spoken too. All students were in and they were all notified of the gathering at night. Ned had to get ready.

From 5 in the afternoon, time was going too fast and Ned was getting desperate for the evening. He finished receiving students in the accommodation office and rushed to his room with his lists of students and their room numbers. First thing he did was to have a bath. He filled the bath and got in it straight away. There was not enough time for anything. He spent a long time scrubbing himself with lynx shower gel and was rehearsing his conversation with Kay, the girl who he really liked and knew would be his. "Hi, I am Ned. You remember me from the office, don't you?" he was talking to himself in the bathroom. "How do you like it here? How is your first day away from home? How about seeing me after this evening?" Ned continued rehearsing. Although he was so used to chatting girls up, on this occasion he could not find the best way to approach this new girl. It was stressful for him and he did not know how to behave. He was in a panic. He was concentrating so much on his approach that he lost track of time. He looked at his watch and it was, to his surprise, 6.30 in the evening. He rushed out of the bath, got in his room and had a close shave although he already had a shave in the morning. This evening was too important to him and he had to be right on his first attempt. It was getting to 7.00 in the evening and time was going even faster. He put his best outfit, a pair of jeans and a dark blue t-shirt. He splashed plenty of aftershave lotion while suffering from the burns at the same time. One could hear his moans and groans from the pain but that was no issue for him. He sprayed plenty of deodorant, brushed his hair back and applied plenty of gel that made his hair look like they were super-glued, wore his 'Nike' trainers bought specially for the occasion and he went to see Shah. He had to have Shah's approval on his looks, as he needed his experience, knowledge and support. In Shah's room he was practising his chat lines. But then he was not comfortable with any of this thought up lines. Shah's advice to him was "be yourself and do not try too hard". Shah got ready and made himself look cool and off they went. Ned asked Shah to reserve a seat for him in the club just in case the club was too packed due to this once a year night. Ned, on the other hand, went room by room to fetch the newcomers and then went to Kay's at the last moment. The rest of the students were waiting outside the building while Ned went to Kay's room. He knocked. He waited for an answer. No reply. He knocked again. A sweet voice with a friendly northern accent replied, "one moment please". Ned was getting shy by the seconds; it was not like him at all. He was sweating and getting impatient as the door still did not open. He knocked again. This time the door opened and Kay said, "I am ready love".

Ned was not used to this type of language. "I am ready love!!!". In Ned's culture love was used only when someone was in love. Confusing! It was for Ned. He, for a moment, went blank in his mind. All sorts of thoughts started going round in his head, "is she already in love with me? She does not even know me, not even my name". Ned was in a muddle while he was staring at Kay in the eyes. Kay broke the silence by touching Ned's hand and said "are you okay, darling?"

"Darling", even more confusing. He was in shock. "You look all pale love, I hope I am not frightening you" said Kay in her sweet voice. She pushed Ned gently out of the way with full body contact and locked her door. She walked ahead while Ned was still in his dream. She came back and got Ned by the arm. "Come on love, let's go" Kay said gently with a large smile in her face. Ned was still in shock while Kay and him walked out of the building. Once outside Ned was talkative to everyone. He introduced himself to the whole group as they walked to the club. In his mind he was confused and troubled. All his excitement turned into fear, that she might not be the person he thought she was yet he was still very attracted to her. He kept looking at her while they were walking and kept bumping into each other. The others were too busy getting to know each other and worrying about the course.

Ned went in the club first and introduced them to the doorman. It was a members' only club and all of them had to sign in. Ned was allowed to sign in for two persons only. So he called Shah to his rescue. Shah, being well-known to the club, got everyone in without interruption. That was Shah's introduction to the students, unplanned yet the best kind of introduction. His ability spoke for him and of course he got chatting straight away. It was amazing. Ned was too much in a shock state that he could not approach Kay although he kept looking or rather staring at her all the time. Ned was asked hundreds of questions about the course and facilities and of course he was offered many drinks in the club that he got merry quickly. But he was not merry enough to have the courage for Kay. Ned was the centre of attention with all those fresh, young, charming and beautiful girls around him. He was the envy of all men in the club. By 11.30 in the evening he was in no state to hold any conversation to anyone and was disappointed with himself that he could not achieve what he set out to do. All the students were still in the club and Ned went to Shah and told him that he could not stand up anymore and that he had to go. Shah offered to escort him to his room but Ned could not be selfish as Shah was having a good time. Ned became popular in one evening with the students but he had to say good-bye, as he had to be fit for college the next morning. He said goodbye to every one of them and went to Kay last. "I would like to apologise that I did not have much time to speak to you, but if you have anything you would like to ask, I do not mind staying few minutes more" Ned said to Kay. "Do not worry about it I am sure we will bump into each other again", Kay replied. Ned said goodbye and goodnight and left the club. He could hardly walk, so he struggled to his room. He was not impressed by his performance. "So many girls, yet no one!" he said to himself. He opened the door and dropped on the floor with the door wide open. He fell asleep. It was a good hour and a half when the rest of the students returned. Few of them were staying in Ned's corridor. When they passed Ned's room they saw him lying down on the floor, fully dressed. It was not difficult to work out what happened there. Ned was too drunk to know anything. The three new girls, Anita, Julie and Carol, dragged him to his bed, and undressed him. They got his pyjamas out and dressed him up for bed, laughing at the same time. They tucked him in warmly and left a note behind him reading, "it was exclusive indeed, looking forward to another night like this, love Anita, Carol and Julie", knowing that he would be embarrassed in the morning. They shut the door behind him and left. Ned slept like a babe, and got up in the morning and adhered to his usual routine. He was brushing his teeth that he suddenly saw the note. He read it and sat on his bed with his toothbrush hanging in his mouth. He was trying to recall what happened. He could not remember anything from the time he came to his room. It was not the pyjamas that he would normally wear as he did not wear any normally. 'Orgasmic night', he did not know what to think. "Not another embarrassing start" he thought. He continued brushing his teeth, "three girls", he thought this time he would definitely not be able to get Kay. He looked in the mirror and smiled and carried on although he was disappointed about his start with Kay. Nevertheless he went to the canteen for breakfast and met all of the students there. Everyone cheered when he got in, needless to say that there was only one seat free and that was with the three girls who left the note for him. He went and sat there for breakfast. He was quiet and everyone was looking at him and laughing and they were having a good time at his expense. He did not mind and talked to them pretending that it was okay. He looked from the corner of his eyes and saw Kay watching him whilst she was talking to her newfound friends. No men on her table, Ned felt quite comfortable with the idea. All the students talked to each other and they all left the canteen together to catch the coach for college. The coach was buzzing inside. They were all anxious which reminded Ned about his first day when he started his nursing course. He smiled as it brought back memories of his first night in the nurse's accommodation being chased by women. Ned was sitting alone for a change and was daydreaming as usual. He was thinking about Kay. She was sitting behind him and he did not even notice. They reached college, Ned went to his lecture and the rest of them went for their orientation and meeting with their tutors. Of course they mentioned how good and helpful Ned was to them in their first day in the nurses home and that made Ned even more welcome among the tutors. Also the tutors knew about Ned's experience with three women and he got the reputation of being the 'stud'. Everyone knew the truth except for Ned. Again everyone had a good laugh but being a strong character he did not let this bother him. His only worry was that he would not be able to get Kay but again he thought that he would give her the time and see if she would go out with anyone else. So he thought he would wait for a week. Kay was never unfriendly to him. They went to college everyday and Ned maintained his routine. No matter how good a time he was having he maintained his principles and he never forgot his purpose in England.

The first week went quickly. Ned did not have much to do with Kay although they were travelling to college in the same coach. Friday came very quick. Returning from college, Kay came to sit next to Ned. He was surprised. They got engaged in a conversation about her school days and his country of birth. It was interesting, as they seemed to get very friendly very quickly; after all they were both easy-going people. Ned was expecting that Kay would ask him about his night with the other girls and to his amazement there was no mention of the subject at all. As they got to the nurses home, they walked towards their rooms together. At the end of the road, they both stood and there were no further conversation. They were looking at each other. Ned did not know what the next move would be as he was a bit shy. "So, are we seeing you in the club tonight?", Kay broke the silence. Ned was in panic. "Sure", he replied, "what time will you be there?", he asked. "After tea and Coronation Street", replied Kay. "Okay, see you in the club later" Ned replied with a smile. They separated and went their own way. Ned carried on with his usual routine and got ready in his own time and went to the club at 10.30 at night. He did not take Kay's invitation too seriously as he did not want to deal with another disappointment again. He got in the club and went straight to Shah to say hello and talked to him about general issues. On the side, Kay was watching Ned. Shah reminded Ned that there was someone who was asking about him and if he did not want to lose his chance he should go there quickly. Ned watched Kay from the corner of his eyes. She was sitting with her friends, with a glass of white wine. Her eyes were constantly checking whether Ned was coming to her or not. On the other hand Ned did not inspire confidence and took his time to go to Kay. Half an hour's chat with Shah and then Ned went to Kay's table. "Hello darling, I thought you would never come. It was getting late and I thought you went to bed already!" exclaimed Kay. "That is my usual time for the club, sorry if I kept you waiting. There is no space here, I will talk to you later" replied Ned. "It is okay, I will stand with you wherever it is convenient" she said. She took her drink and they stood next to the bar. Meanwhile everyone's eye was on both of them as Kay was a really stunning girl, gorgeous and curvy, and as many would put it, delicious and orgasmic. Kay and Ned were talking to each other, talking about anything and everything except about going out. All dialogues were turning towards education and nursing. Kay was trying to change the subject to movies and meals but Ned was too slow to pick up the hints. Shah called Ned before leaving and whispered, "one can tell she is yours for keeping, good luck man". They hugged as usual before separating. That was a sign of respect and brotherhood for them. Ned came back to Kay. "You two seem to be good mates" she commented. "Yeah, Shah is my brother and we know each other for a year now", replied Ned. Ned told Kay about their trip to Lake District and their camping experience. They laughed till the end of the night. The bell rang announcing last orders. Ned offered Kay her last drink and he got a coke for himself as he did not like getting drunk as he did not want to lose control of the situation, although he knew he was not doing very well controlling the situation. Then Kay asked Ned about the chase in the middle of the night the previous year. Ned was not embarrassed anymore and told her what happened the first night he was in the nurse's home. To this question he thought another question would be about the session with her classmates. However, Kay did not ask this question and just gave him a pleasant smile to make him feel comfortable. They talked to each other but they did not have any body contact. The club announced the closing time and they all left the club. Ned and Kay left together. When they got out Kay said, "it is a beautiful night, Ned". "Yeah, beautiful indeed. It is a shame that it has to finish so quickly" said Ned. They walked towards their rooms and then, Ned took the courage and said "can I come for a cup of tea?". "I have no tea" replied Kay. "Do you have a kettle?" asked Ned. "Yes", replied Kay. Ned put his hands in his pocket and got two tea bags out and said, "here you are. I hope there is water!". "mmm, very original" said Kay. And they both got in her room. Kay made tea and they both continued talking about the studies again. It was getting late and Kay said she was tired, hinting that Ned should leave. Ned was chivalrous, he apologised for the intrusion and keeping her awake. Kay said, "sorry darling I do not mean it that way. I am really tired". She came to Ned and knelt on the floor. She opened his legs and got in the middle. Meanwhile Ned started to shiver. He did not have such situation before and did not know the procedure. So he just kept quiet and stood up. Kay stood with him and he said, "so good night and I will see you tomorrow if you want". Kay did not reply to this, she held Ned by his face and kissed him on the lips. Ned was in shock and started shaking. He stopped for a long minute and looked at her in the eyes. She kissed him again. He stopped and this time he took the courage and kissed her back, and, that was a long French kiss. There were no speech and he left.

Ned smiled all the way to his room. He was so excited that he studied until very late that night. It gave him extra energy. He was positive indeed. He went for breakfast in the morning and met Kay. They sat on the same table and went to college together. They sat together in the bus. Returning from college they talked about many different things except about what happened the previous night. Ned thought he would let things happen in its own time and was under no circumstances going to put any pressure. When they reached home, Kay invited Ned for tea at 7.00 in the evening. Ned was excited and went to his room straight away and got on with his studies. He had a bath and went to see Shah to share his good news. Shah was ecstatic with the news. Shah and Ned went to the canteen for dinner and then they went their own way. Ned went to his room and got ready to visit Kay in her room. He put on his best underwear and outfit, fit to impress. He strolled along the path to meet Kay. He knocked at the door and was welcomed in. To his surprise there were several girls in the room. Ned was rather confused. He did not know what to make of it. They got chatting and Ned was there sitting and desperately waiting for his cup of tea. One by one, Kay's friends left the room leaving just the two of them. Ned assumed that something was about to happen. So he waited patiently and waited. Meanwhile Kay was changing her college outfit in front of him and putting on something else. Ned was getting more and more anxious during that time. "What is this?", he thought. Kay definitely had a good-looking, trim and curvy body fit enough to kill him in one night. Looking at Kay getting changed was raising his temperature. He did not know where to look and his trousers were bulging which was very hard to hide from anyone's eyesight. He tried his best not to embarrass himself. He excused himself and went to the toilet to cool himself down. He was quite a long time in there as he was trying to erase what he saw from his mind. He came back after fifteen minutes and stood at the door. Meanwhile the rest of Kay's friends came to her room and were standing and waiting. Ned was getting impatient, as he was addicted to tea. Ned said, "okay, I will make a move ladies". Kay turned around and said "wait darling, we are all going for tea". This tea business was getting out of Ned's hand. So he thought he did not know what is going on and he had to play the game. Ten minutes later they were all ready and Kay came out and shut the door and they all started walking out. Ned followed. Very odd type of tea that was!. Ned followed them to the canteen. In the canteen Ned told Kay that he already had his dinner. "I thought I mentioned that you were invited for tea!" Kay exclaimed. Ned was more surprised and explained, "sorry, you asked me to come for tea and I was there for a cup tea and I don't know why I have to come to the canteen for tea". Kay smiled and holding his hand she explained, "by tea, I meant tea in the evening". Ned was in a puzzle, "but I came for tea…" said Ned. To that, one of Kay's friend explained that tea meant having evening meal. Ned did not know what to say. "There is a lack of communication and … understanding here", said Ned. The whole thing about tea was beginning to get complicated. "For me breakfast is in the morning, lunch is at noon and dinner is in the evening, and tea is a cup of tea which I have been waiting for, for a long time", said Ned. They all started laughing and Kay asked Ned to sit with them while they were having their tea. From then on tea and dinner became a standard joke. Ned being stubborn, left the canteen, as he was not at ease about sitting there for nothing, he would rather go back and do some studies. He returned and went straight to Shah, explained him the situation and from then onwards Shah taught Ned about the different expressions and swear words and all Ned needed to know in order to be able to go out with Kay. Life was complicated enough without having to learn the dialect and colloquial English. But he had to do it in order not to be ridiculed. He stayed with Shah until 9.30 in the night when Shah was leaving for the club. Ned had enough waiting for tea and being laughed at so he decided to go back to his room and do his own things for the rest of the night. When he came down to his surprise he saw a note on his door, "came to see you, but you were out. Waiting for you. Kay". He ignored the note and got in his room. He changed and got on with his studies. Time went very quickly. It was midnight when suddenly there was a knock on his door. "Who could it be at this time, I hope it is not Mary", and Ned opened the door. "This is unusual" Ned said, "come on in... enter my palace". Kay walked in and looked at Ned's room. "Very tidy" said Kay. She sat on the bed and looked at Ned. "What can I do for you", said Ned coldly. "I just came to visit you if it is okay" replied Kay. "Of course it is okay, would you like tea ... or a cup of tea", asked Ned. To that they both broke down in laughter. "A lovely hot cup of tea will do", replied Kay laughingly. From then on they started talking to each other. They both apologised to each other for the lack of understanding and communication and they got on all right. Kay stayed until she finished her tea and gave Ned a skilful kiss and left as she said she was tired. Ned complimented Kay on her kisses and said, ''your kisses are delicious and sweet, and I enjoy them''. Kay made no comments and left. Ned continued to study with a large smile in his face and then went to sleep.

8

Next evening Ned and Kay met again after the club. They had a cup of tea and they started kissing each other. This time it was the real thing. The kisses were longer. They were both getting hot and started cuddling each other in bed. Ned did not have any high expectations as every step of his has been rather disastrous, so he let go with the flow. Kay took Ned's shirt off and kissed his chest and nipples. It was exciting. Ned was moaning with pleasure. She kept doing that for a while and went down to his trousers, undid his buttons one by one and kissing every inch of his exposed body. She dragged his trousers down slowly and gently while kissing and biting his thighs. The underwear was untouched. Shirt off, trousers off, and socks off. Ned was then confident to do his bit. He threw Kay down on the bed and kissed her all over her face and neck. The moans of pleasure was getting louder and louder. He unbuttoned her shirt off and kissed her on the bra and her belly. He took a bite now and then when she moved. He kissed her beautiful body and delicious skin non-stop while he pulled her jeans down. He admired her trim legs. Needless to say that there was a big bulge in his underwear ready for action. Kay was left in her bra and knickers. Her eyes were closed all the time as she was in high heavens. Ned turned her over so that she was lying on her stomach. He moved her hair away from her neck and started kissing her just below her hair on the neck. Kay could not breathe with pleasure with her body moving up and down in a rhythm. Ned went down to her spine and then to her bra. He tried to undo it but no luck. It was getting harder to undo it when Kay's arms just went round her back and offered assistance. That action built his confidence, but again he did not want to take anything for granted. Ned kissed her thighs and waist and knickers-line then turned her facing him. She opened her eyes and looked at him and one could see that she was getting desperate to get closer to Ned. Ned gently lowered himself on her and rubbed his chest on hers kissing her lips at the same time. They were both getting desperate for each other, rolling on the single bed from side to side and moaning and groaning with pleasure, they were both having the best time of their life. Kay was stroking Ned's bulge and then she gently pushed her little hands inside holding the real things. She moaned when she felt the inside package and stroke the whole length. She kept feeling the circumference and the length in order to know the size. She grabbed Ned tightly and pulled him near, showing that she appreciated the package. Ned was sweating with agony and desperation. They had been at it for about an hour. Ned got up and opened Kay legs and lowered himself in the middle and rubbed his package on hers and pushed harder at the same time ensuring that he did not hurt her. It was his first time and he did not exactly know how to go about things and was waiting for Kay's moves. Kay gathered that Ned was a virgin and that excited her even more, so she put her hands forward and pushed his underwear down to his thighs. Ned did the same to her and then Kay helped by pulling her knickers down and out all the way. There was Ned at the brink of losing his virginity. Kay grabbed him tight on the waist and enjoyed the motion. This time Ned attempted to slide his manhood in Kay's wet and slippery passage. Suddenly Kay stopped and asked, "have you got a condom?". "No", replied Ned. "In that case we better leave it for the next time, I would rather be safe than sorry" said Kay. "That is okay by me, but that does not mean we have to stop, it is still pleasing to cuddle", said Ned. "It is exquisite, but I know what is going to happen afterwards" replied Kay. To this she got up and put her pyjamas on. She offered Ned another cup of tea and then got in bed. Ned was sitting in bed and was looking at Kay falling asleep. Ned did not have time to finish his tea that Kay was already sleeping. He spent the next fifteen minutes looking at her in her sleep and admiring her beauty. She looked so kind and gentle and innocent, she looked like she could not hurt anyone even if she tried. There was so much peace. Ned finished his tea and got a pen and paper to leave a note.

'Dear Kay,
Thank you for having me tonight. You are the best thing that ever happened to me. To let you know that I will be thinking of you until I see you next time. I would like to see you in the party on Saturday night. I will be in Cornwall with some friends and hope to be back by 8.00 in the evening, in time for the party. See you in the canteen in the morning.
Ned.'

Ned went to his room, euphoric that the ice was broken and he knew that he had someone to go to. In his room, first thing he did was to take his schedule out. He planned his studies time and socialising hours and Kay's time. All was included and also he had his allocated time for personal space and for thinking, and daydreaming. He completed his plan and stuck it on the wall and went to bed, satisfied.

9

The week went fast and Ned did not see very much of Kay as he was on practical learning. However, on Friday, he went to Cornwall to be back for Saturday. It was a long distance drive with friends especially for one night clubbing in the country. The evening in Cornwall was good but he was missing Kay. What was bothering him most was that he might lose her as he has not seen her for some time. They left Cornwall on Saturday at 4.00 in the afternoon in order to be back in time for the party in the club. The drive was slow due to an accident on the motorway. Ned was pressuring David to drive faster but that was no good. The traffic was just the same. The others wanted to be in the club for the party as well. They were all getting desperate. Driving at average speed would not get them in the club in time so they decided to drive non-stop missing their comfort stop. That was agreed by all and they continued with music rocking the car. It was still a good trip. On the M4, past Reading, Ned was getting desperate to use the toilet. Nobody wanted to stop. So, John emptied the bottle of coke on the motorway and handed it to Ned. Ned had to squeeze himself in the packed car and use the bottle while the others were making a joke of it. Needless to say that it became a standard joke for the rest of his training. He managed it and he emptied the bottle on the road. They kept going as fast as they could. They reached home at 9.30 in the evening. All of them got out of the car and ran to their rooms. Ned was the most desperate of all, he did not tell anyone of his date with Kay. He got in the bath, got ready and ran to the club at 10.30. As soon as he got in he saw Kay. She was sitting on a table with the other students and there were men all around trying to chat them up, including Kay. Ned thought he lost his chance and went straight to the bar to get a drink. At the bar Shah was sitting on the stool at his usual place. They talked to each other and shared the latest information and developments in the club. Shah also told Ned that Kay has been asking about him and that she was waiting for him even if it took all night for him to get back. To that Ned felt reassured and went to see Kay. There was no space for Ned. Seeing Ned, Kay made her way to him and they stood together talking for a while. Kay looked at him and smiled saying, "I have been waiting for you for a long time, darling". She did not give him a chance to reply and asked him about his trip as a general conversation. They talked to each other. Then Ned asked Kay for a dance, and it was not a slow dance either. It was all hip gyrating and sexy music that Ned liked dancing to. He took Kay and swung her on the dance floor. They were dancing passionately that anyone watching would think they were having sex on the dance floor. When they were dancing, one by one everyone stopped dancing and watched their co-ordinated dance movement. It was something everyone was envious of, not only the dance but of Ned and Kay. They were still together for the first, second and third dance when one of Kay's friends asked Ned to dance with her. That was the start of interruption that kept each other away from dancing together all night. One by one all new students in the club danced what they called 'Ned's bed dance' with Ned. All men in the club got envious of Ned. And at one point Ned had five girls dancing close to him and they even tried undressing him on the dance floor. It was a great night. Ned became famous for his dance that no one could ever imitate. At 01.00 in the morning the party was over, everyone was drunk except for Kay. She was sitting there watching Ned all the time. She always maintained her smile and no rude word to anyone. When the club was closing Ned came to her and said, "come on, lets go". Kay put her arms around his waist and they walked to Ned's room zigzagging all the way. Ned was drunk beyond control. So, having known his previous record with women when he was drunk, Kay stayed the night in his room to protect him from further mishaps, disaster and ridicule. She undressed him and put him to bed. She sat there looking at him for a long time. The single bed was no bed for two people. She watched him snoring and took pleasure of that moment when he was not serious, not thinking about anything else and not worrying. This was rare for anyone to see and Kay treasured this moment and she knew Ned was hers for a long time and she knew that no matter how many girls would try to get him in bed he would always come home to her bed. She was not worried about getting in a relationship with him; he was so innocent and peaceful in his sleep. Kay left his room around 03.00 in the morning and went to sleep.

Ned slept till late on Sunday. He got up afterward and continued his day as scheduled. He did not see Kay the whole day, as he had to get on with his study as planned. Kay on the other side knew from Shah that Ned had a schedule, which he would not leave. So at 7.00 in the evening Kay went to see Ned for a cup of tea. Ned was busy with his books. So, he offered Kay a cup of tea and went back to his studies making an occasional conversation. Kay was looking at him all the time and she was admiring his devotion and commitment to his aim in life. She somehow did not mind. She finished her tea and asked, "I know you are busy darling, and I would not dream of disturbing you. I will see you when you finish if it is okay". Ned looked as his schedule and replied, "mmm... I have few things to do. I would like to see you but there is no point coming when while being with you I will be thinking of things I have not done. I cannot be with you and be feeling guilty. So, how about tomorrow night?". "Tomorrow night it is, darling. Would you like wine instead of tea?" asked Kay. "That is thoughtful. How about making it into a special night?" suggested Ned. "How?", asked Kay. "How about going for meal to a posh restaurant? And afterwards I would like to give you my virginity!" suggested Ned. "This sounds great. What time shall I be ready for you?" asked Kay. "9.30 will be good" replied Ned. Kay kissed him on his forehead and left the room. Ned continued his works.

10

The next afternoon, Ned went to Shah and got some tips about making the evening extravagant. He got some ideas about what to wear and where to go for a tasty Indian meal. Shah helped Ned to relax and built his confidence by just talking to him. He also gave Ned some condoms. Ned left Shah and went to get ready. He put on his suit and Davidoff cool water aftershave, gelled his hair and went to the local shop that was within walking distance. He bought a dozen of red roses and brought them back to his room discreetly. He rested in his room and did his works fully dressed for the evening until 9.30. He went to Kay on time. He knocked the door at 9.30 precisely. Kay opened the door straightaway. She looked stunning in her black dress and full make-up. Her hair was curly and expertly done. She looked one in a million for the evening. Ned stared at her full of joy and presented the bunch of rose to her from behind his back. Kay looked at them in surprise and smiled. She glowed with happiness. She took them and gave Ned a heavenly kiss on the lips and said, "they are so beautiful, thank you". She arranged them in a vase and they left for the restaurant. They walked to the restaurant hand in hand. It was a wonderful evening. They both looked as if they were made for each other. They walked gently, no rush. They could not keep their hands away from each other, holding hands, then holding waist, then holding shoulders. They arrived at the restaurant after 20 minutes walk.

They sat in the restaurant in the most romantic place and ordered their meal. Kay never tried Indian food before and Ned had to recommend the recipes that were not hot. They also ordered a bottle of white wine. They chatted their way throughout the meal. It was a very beautiful evening. They were getting merry drinking the wine. They had a full course meal and enjoyed it thoroughly. Ned offered to pay the entire amount and would not have Kay pay for anything. She insisted but Ned was a gentleman and would not have it. They left the restaurant around midnight and walked hand in hand towards the hospital. It was a beautiful evening with full moon to complement it. They strolled along walking side by side and enjoying each other's company. The return home was peaceful and quiet. They did not talk at all. It was just satisfying being with each other. Coming near the nurse's accommodation, Kay pulled Ned towards her and they started kissing gently. It was long and passionate and both would have wished that moment to last a lifetime. Afterwards, they walked to Kay's room. Kay led from then onward, as she knew that Ned was the shy type and she also knew that he was a virgin. In the room, Ned sat on the armchair whilst Kay took the wine out of the fridge. Ned opened it with his expertise, spilling wine everywhere on the carpet. This was a funny situation as they were both merry with the wine. Ned poured the wine with Kay sitting on his lap. The wine remained there whilst they started kissing each other gently. One by one Ned took Kay's dress and underwear off until she was naked. It was a very sexy sight with Kay's striking and curvy body shining with the dim light. Ned was reluctant to take his clothing off. So Kay got to work. She had some more wine and encouraged Ned to drink so that he would be more relaxed. They drank the whole bottle whilst Kay was naked and whilst she was kissing him on his neck and shoulders. She had to take action therefore she pulled Ned on to her bed and turned the lights off. She gently kissed Ned while taking his shirt and trousers off. It was romantic, no rush, and plenty of time. She went down to his underwear and pulled it down gently stroking his bulge. It was huge and more than a handful. She looked rather satisfied with that and continued until she gently lowered her lips to that area kissing him gently. Ned was relaxed and moaned with pleasure. The moans were getting louder and louder when Kay suddenly stopped and rolled on top of him. He was getting desperate and held Kay tightly next to him. They rolled on top of each other for a long while, playing with each other's sexual parts and exciting each other beyond belief. Ned gently pushed Kay on the bed so that she was lying flat on her back and started doing the same as she did to him. He stroked her breast and sucked her nipples until they were erect and kissed her every inch on the body until he reached the groins. He expertly lowered his tongue in between her legs and gave her the best time of her life that Kay was moaning and groaning until she had a long orgasm. That was not enough, Ned continued until Kay called for him to stop and asked him to penetrate. To that instruction, Ned did not waste time, he took the condom out of his trousers that was lying next to him and Kay assisted him to put it on. He lowered his hips in the middle of Kay's legs but could not find the place where to place it. Kay confidently held his manhood and guided it slowly in her vagina, moaning with pleasure at the same time. They stayed in that position all the time with Ned pushing in and out gently until Kay had a second multiple orgasm. He continued. They were both sweating until the bed sheets were wet, but they continued. Ned and Kay were both moaning and groaning which was getting louder and louder until the neighbour next door started banging on the wall. They smiled to each other and quietened down but continued. Ned was nowhere near his orgasm while Kay was getting tired. She had to make him cum. So she turned over and guided Ned from behind. She was now on doggy style and pushing harder and harder into Ned. Suddenly Ned started shuddering and started pushing with his entire force. Kay was screaming on top of her voice while the next-door neighbour was banging harder on to the wall. But they were too far-gone and could not hear anything but enjoying the moment. The bed was squeaking and knocking on to the wall. It was satisfactorily noisy. Ned's pushes were getting stronger and stronger and Kay could not cope anymore. She was shouting to Ned to cum quick. Finally he came and expired the loudest groan he ever expired before and collapsed on top of Kay's back. Kay remained there, flat in bed, on cloud nine and enjoying the moment while Ned was trying to catch his breath. They both fell asleep as they were. On the other side the neighbour stopped banging the wall. Everything was suddenly quiet. They finally moved away from that position and held on to each other and continued to sleep.

In the morning they both woke up with a knock on the door. Ned got out of bed half asleep and went to open the door. He did not realise that he was not in his bedroom as he never slept in someone else's room before. All innocently he opened the door to see Kay's girlfriend standing at the door. Susan started laughing when she saw Ned. All embarrassed, Ned did not know what to make of it. He looked down at what Susan was staring at and saw himself in Kay's underwear. He could not work out how he got in it. He looked back and found Kay in his underwear. By then Susan also noticed what Ned looked at in all amazement. Kay started laughing. Ned banged the door shut and wrapped the towel around him whilst Kay got herself wrapped in her bed sheet. Kay then answered the door to Susan and they went to talk in the kitchen. They were giggling to themselves. Meanwhile Ned tried to recall the events of the night and smiled to himself. He did it finally. After few minutes Kay came back and gave Ned a big kiss and said how wonderful the night was for her. They got dressed afterwards and Kay made an unexpected breakfast and they planned to meet again. They both looked fulfilled and knew that they were going to see each other for a long time. Ned went to his room and did his usual things and at night he went to the club with Kay. Of course, by then the entire club knew the events of the previous night due to the noisy activity. They all had a good laugh at Ned's expense and had a drink. Ned met Shah and they shared their usual opinions of recent occurrences and updated with home news. After the club Kay and Ned went to their rooms and they met late at night after Ned finished with his studies. Again they had the most beautiful and romantic time together. From that night onwards Kay was permanently introduced in Ned's schedule. They met every night, religiously.

On and off Kay invited Ned for dinner in her room and she made the best chicken casserole until Ned got in the kitchen with her and they started making curried chicken casserole. They both enjoyed their invented meals, European and Asian recipes mixed together. They compromised in many other things as they were growing in their relationship. Sex was the best thing. There was not a single night they would spend without it. They tried all sorts of unusual techniques and food items such as yoghurts and chocolates to spice things up. They also bought a Karma sutra book which they studied together and tried all the different positions on evenings. Their passion was becoming envy for other men and women in the hospital. There was not anyone who did not know about Ned and Kay and their being together. Lots of people tried to plan temptations to separate their desire for each other but were unsuccessful. Kay would let Ned out to clubs and discos with Shah or other friends and would not worry about him sleeping with anyone else, as she knew Ned well enough. She always maintained that no matter whom Ned danced with or kissed on the dance floor, in the end of the day he would come to her bed. That was very true of Ned and they trusted each other. Ned would have lots of girls flirting with him all night, each one wanting her share of the sexy dance and a snog and each one trying to woo him in bed, but in his heart and soul there was only one person, Kay. Also Ned believed that true love was in freedom. He never pressured Kay in any way. She would do her own things with her friend's and Ned did not mind at all. Yet they would go to the club and join in entertainments. They did not cut off with friends from the club and friends from college. They were both popular. Their love life went well from September until Christmas holiday.

11

Kay, being from England was planning to go home for Christmas same like everyone else except for those like Ned and Shah. Ned was not pleased, as this was the first time that he had been in a relationship. It was not about jealousy as they were really fond of each other but it was about being alone. Ned went to see Shah about the issue. After discussing it for a long time Shah realised that Ned was in love and did not know about it. He expressed his thought to Ned who did not believe it himself. But one thing he knew was that he already started missing Kay, and she had not even gone yet, she was only planning.

Ned went to see Kay straight away and asked her how she felt about him. Kay told him that she was fond of him and would not exchange him for anything. He then asked her about her plan for her holidays. Kay outlined her plans. She was going to her parents to spend Christmas and that she would leave after the last day at college and would come back the Sunday before the start of the semester. For Kay it was something normal and she did not realise that those who have no families were staying in the nurse's accommodation and most often opted to work so that they kept themselves busy.

Ned wished her joyous times with her parents and said nothing to upset Kay as to her it was something normal. From the time they talked about the Christmas holiday Ned missed Kay a lot although they spent a lot of time together. Their lovemaking was more passionate than ever. Kay did not understand what was happening to Ned and enjoyed every moment they spent together.

The day arrived when Kay had to leave for home. She had to travel by train from Euston, as her parents could not fetch her. So Ned offered to accompany her with her suitcase and her hand luggage to Euston. They were both quiet. Kay was thinking about meeting her parents and her sister and how exciting it would be to get together again as that was the first time she had been away from home. She had a lot of imagination in her head and occasionally she would give a smile while looking out of the window. Sitting next to her, Ned was patiently accompanying her with lots of sadness, which Kay never noticed. His heart was crying out for her not to go but he could not be selfish after all he was the new boyfriend she only knew about three months ago. He tackled this issue in his head and decided to show no emotion on her departure and set her off with a big smile so that she would go with this positive smile to treasure when she would be thinking of him at home. They got to the station and just as the train departure time was announced, Ned took out a small packet out of his jacket pocket and handed it over to Kay. "I hope you have the best Christmas and do not forget to call me every now and then" said Ned and gave her a heavenly kiss. Kay was surprised and gave him the longest meaningful hug she had ever given to anybody. "I will miss you, darling" replied

Kay. "I know you will but have a good time anyway" Ned commented and smiled. "You cockey bugger", she said. They kissed and as Ned planned, he waved good-bye with a big smile. So that was Kay, gone away for 14 days. He watched Kay disappear in the crowd going for the train. He waited on the bench until the train had gone. He was sitting and thinking. Ned has never been so passionate before and had never missed anyone so much before. He accepted that he was in love with Kay but what could he do? They were from different culture and race. He thought he would keep being the man for her and he missed her so much. Sadness was showing on his face as if he would break down in tears any minute. Few minutes after the train left he got up and started his return journey home. Ned came back from Euston and went straight to bed as it was late and he was tired and was not in a mood to do anything.

Kay, on the other hand, slept on her way back and had to change train three times until she reached home at 23.45 at night. Her mother opened the door and Kay was greeted back home with lots of love and tears. She was hugged by her family that consisted of mum, dad and sister. They sat for few minutes in the middle of the night sharing their experiences of life without family members. Kay was careful about mentioning anything about Ned as she knew her family would react badly to it. They had tea and cakes and her parents retired to bed while Kay went for a long and well deserved bath. She took her entire time to settle down in the bath. By accident her eyesight went on the clock and she started thinking about the time she spent with Ned at that time of the night every night. She missed him and she knew he missed her too. She felt the urge to call him but did not as she did not want to disturb him at that time of the night and most of all she did not want her parents to suspect anything of that kind. She was getting desperate to talk to Ned. So, after the bath, out of desperation she opened his Christmas present. In the box, she found a little bear wrapped in a piece of paper with a message from Ned on it. It read as follows,

"To you my sweetheart,
I had the most wonderful time with you.
May be, it is different for you,
But for me is just wonderful and even more.
It has been great knowing you, and being with you.
You make me feel complete and with you around I do not need anyone else.
With you I am one. Without you, I am none.
I will wait for you patiently and although I never say it, I miss you now and will miss you when you are gone.
There will be an empty space waiting to be filled when you come back.

Enjoy Christmas with your family and send them my best regards and wishes.

May your wish come true. Happy Christmas and also a happy New Year.

If you open this present before Christmas, then I will know about it, as I will feel it when you really miss me.

From someone very dear to you."

After reading this note from Ned, Kay's eyes were full of tears as she missed him. Worst of all was that she would not be able to share her happiness with Ned with anyone in the family. She was full of sadness that she fell asleep thinking about Ned. She was indeed over the moon with him and she knew it as well as Ned.

Kay got up late in the morning and went downstairs for breakfast. They kissed each other good-morning and sat at the table. They were like before talking about their previous day and the day in front of them. There was nothing abnormal except for Kay. She was thinking of Ned all the time. Her days at her parents went by visiting old friends and relatives and catching up with her social life. She was having a great time and as the days went by she was missing Ned more and more. She did not dare call him as she did not want to create any problems at home and wanted her Christmas to be memorable. Meanwhile Ned's holidays went by going to the cinema and jogging. He went to the social club every night with Shah and he was noticed to be alone by everyone. In the club there were disco's almost every night due to the festive season and Ned had lots of offers and temptations to go with other girls but he stuck to the one he loved although she was absent. He did his usual dancing and joining in all sorts of late night room parties and sex games but went to his bed on his own every night. His loyalty to Kay was remarkable. He was there, alone, and all the girls wanted that opportunity to spend at least one night with him. However, he belonged to someone else.

Time went slowly for Ned being bored on his own and missing Kay. He used this time to do some extra work on his studies and prepared for forthcoming assignments and made various plans for his studies. He did not waste time sulking. Meanwhile Kay was busy with the festive seasons and preparations for the 25th of December. On the eve Kay was at home with her family and was very quiet. Her dad asked her whether there was anything she wanted to talk about. She declined the offer and said that she was okay and just tired. So she went to bed early. In bed, she could not sleep. She was suffering and was in pain. Love hurts. Her parents knew nothing of it and they went to bed. In the nurses home Ned was having a good time with Shah and the rest of those who stayed back to work and those who had nowhere to go. They were all drunk and singing along. They made enough noise for the whole of the village. It was a great night in the club. They were like a big family having fun that went up to early hours of the 25th. They all greeted and kissed in their drunkenness. The club closed after 3 in the morning. Shah and Ned left and struggled to their rooms and collapsed in bed. They were not seen for the whole day. They were recovering from their drinking night. No regrets though, they enjoyed it at the time.

On the other side of England, Kay got up in the morning and helped her mum while her dad and her sister were still sleeping. Her mother and herself talked a lot about various things and she was questioned about boyfriend. Kay ignored that particular question and no further inquires were made. Her mother knew straight away there was something but kept quiet, as she knew Kay was old enough to make her decisions. However, she was surprised at being closed to her as Kay was always open to dialogue about boyfriends in the past. Nevertheless, nothing further was discussed then onwards. Kay, her parents and sister sat for lunch and shared their Christmas presents and were truly having a good time. They were having their lunch and as usual roast Turkey was on the menu. After lunch they were all drunk and then they went to the lounge to continue the afternoon with games. Kay's friends visited as she was in town and they caught up on recent development. Every friend of hers was talking about his/her latest relationship. The talk about relationship started Kay off. She suddenly realised how much she missed Ned. She was wondering what he was up to. She was thinking how and whom he was spending his festive season with. It all started coming to her in a flash. She felt like going to see him straight away and kiss and cuddle him and wish him happy Christmas, but that was not feasible. She kept socialising at home until all the visitors went one by one. Her parents and herself were still in the lounge having wine and talking. Kay on the other hand put on a brave face and maintained the smile. By 9.00 in the evening, it was becoming unbearable and she suddenly got up, excused herself, and told her mum she had to use the phone to call the nurse's home. Kay's mum was not surprised as she felt that there was something behind Kay's behaviour. The phone was in the corridor next door and Kay went. She shut the door behind her and dialled Ned's number in the nurse's home. As there were few nurses and student nurses staying behind Ned answered the phone. "Merry Christmas, darling. You won't believe how much I missed you!" said Kay. "Same to you, Kay. I hope you liked your present. I miss you too....", replied Ned that he could hear Kay's mum's voice asking her no to be too long as she was waiting for a phone call from her sister. Kay, disappointedly, said to Ned that she had to go. Their conversation on the phone did not last longer than one minute but they both felt better after that as they could express their feelings for one another even though just for a minute. After the phone call Ned went to his room and continued with his studies and went to the club as usual.

Whereas for Kay, her mum and dad happened to hear her conversation with Ned. Straight away, as soon as Kay walked in the lounge, she was questioned. "Who was that you were talking to Kay?" asked her mum. "It was Ned, a friend from college. He is staying back, so I thought I would send him my greetings", replied Kay. "Is it a serious relationship" asked her dad. "He is a very good friend, dad", replied Kay and she cleverly terminated the discussion. She, very strongly, felt that this discussion was not at its end. Kay's mother and father looked at each other. They did not know who Ned was and where he came from and what his family background was. They did not have the slightest idea that he was not English. Anyhow, Kay's parents had a long talk prior to going to bed and they did not find anything wrong in Kay having a very good friend although they assumed that it could be something more. They also set Kay's sister off to find out more about this Ned bloke and how far Kay was into him. After her parents went to bed, Kay and her sister had a long talk about various things and about life in the nurse's home and studies. Her sister talked about her boyfriend and his visit to their home and all sorts of things. Kay knew her family well and she knew exactly where her sister was coming from. So she tackled her and asked her if their parents were worried about her friendship with Ned. The reply she got was exactly what she was expecting, her parents were worried and it was not from being selfish but because they were a close family and they loved each other very much and they protected each other very much too. They did not want her to get hurt. Kay was careful about the information she gave to her sister about Ned. All she told her sister was that he was a good friend and that he was helpful and that they go to college together, very basic things. Her sister could not get anything out of Kay. After a long talk they retired to bed. Kay was lying down, mixed up. What should she do? If they get the slightest hint that he was a foreigner they would faint. So she had to bear the pain and went to sleep. As long as they did not know that she was going out with him, nothing mattered as she was strong enough to cope with the situation. After that night Kay called Ned only once from a public phone and they had a good heart to heart chat which made them feel better. New year came and again Kay called Ned from outside the house so that her parents would not doubt anything. As it was, they did not doubt anything and they were quite relaxed with Kay and her choice for studying to be a nurse. New year started well. On the other side of life, Ned also had a good beginning of the New Year with Shah and the rest of people in the club.

12

When the holidays were over Kay came back from home all by herself as her parents could not drive her back on that particular Sunday. As expected Ned went to pick Kay up from the station in London. Meeting Kay at the station was so exciting. They were both impatient. Time was not moving fast enough for them. As soon as train arrived, Kay started looking for Ned and Ned was jumping up and down trying to locate Kay. They finally saw each other and they ran and met with a long hug followed by a deep kiss. They missed each other very much. From the time they met they did not take their hands off one another. They kept close to each other all the time. They did not want to be apart any longer. They knew they were in love. They came to the nurse's home and settled down. No pressure, so Ned went back to his room and asked Kay to join him when she was rested and was ready. Kay settled down and after 3 hours she went to see Ned. She brought a bottle of wine with her. They stayed lying down in bed and talking for a long time and drinking the wine. Kay did not tell Ned anything about her parents and the questions as she did not want to upset him but she was ready to keep him for as long as she could although that would involve a lot of lying to her parents. After the wine they went for a walk to the park and came back feeling good and refreshed.

They were away from each other for the first time and they were dying to go to bed. Coming back to the nurse's home Kay asked Ned to come to her room and suggested that she would give him the best action that he had ever known. No need to say that Kay used yoghurt, chocolate, cream and strawberry to make the night eventful. It was the best night Kay and Ned ever had. They shared a lot of bedroom fantasies and lots of sexual desires that only made their relationship stronger. They explored each other to the maximum. Sex was a strong part of their relationship but the most important part of the relationship was communication. They could talk for hours at a time and always kissing, holding hands and complimenting. The beauty of their relationship was extravagant. They were the 'item' in the nurse's home, and the envy one was envious of. Following the holidays, Kay's next visit home would be for Easter. So her parents called her and said they were visiting her in February.

13

When Kay got the confirmation that her parents would be visiting her for a weekend she was worried and restless. She had one month to prepare for their arrival. That meant she had time to talk to her friends about her relationship with Ned. She had to tell anyone who would be involved in entertaining her parents that any questions about Ned must be ignored and if persisted then they had to convey the same message that they were friends. She also had to reserve a room for them from the nurse's accommodation officer. That was not difficult compared to talking to her friends as there would be questions about the reasons for doing so. From the time she knew they were coming to the day they arrived Kay was prepared. However, Ned only knew about her preparation the day before. At that time Ned got stressed as he felt that there was something drastically wrong. Kay had to assure Ned that it was only a precautionary measure as they were a very close family and she did not want to stress her parents. Ned was not convinced but was buoyant with the arrangement. He assured Kay that he would not see her on the weekend in her room and that he would pretend to be a friend during that period. After all Ned would do anything for Kay as he loved her dearly. On the other hand he was not sure as to why Kay would withhold their relationship to her family as he did not have any problems with his parents.

The weekend in February arrived. Ned stayed out of sight and out of the way. And to do that he kept himself in his room and continued with his studies. Meanwhile Kay's parents arrived in the nurse's home in the afternoon after a long drive. They brought for her a television and few other things to make her life comfortable. They all sat down in her room and had tea and coffee and enjoyed a rest prior to going to the town centre. They took a pleasant and easy walk to town and did some shopping and walked around. They wanted to know more about the area Kay was living in. Whilst walking back they came across Peter who was also a student nurse but living in a different nurse's home. Kay introduced Peter to her parents and first question from Peter was the whereabouts of Ned. Kay tried to escape from the question and told him that Ned has gone out with Shah. They finished their conversation and Peter continued with his trip to the underground train station. Kay's parents looked at each other when Ned was mentioned. He was talked about although he was not around. Kay's father said that he would like to meet this famous Ned. He was a good friend of their daughter and they wanted to meet him. So Kay was asked to introduce Ned. She got worried and told them that after their return she would check if he would be in or perhaps would like to come to the club in the evening. Kay's parents were persistent that they would like to meet him and so it was agreed, and Kay had no choice. However, she did not make a big issue with this in order not to cause any hassle. So when they got back, Kay left her parents in her room and ran to Ned. She told him about the situation and suggested that Ned would meet them in the club. That was agreed and Kay left quickly not to create any suspicion. She came back and settled down with her parents. Ned, at this stage was very naïve about some British or English attitude towards foreigners. He came from a country where he grew up in a multiracial, multicultural and close community. So he went to see Shah to talk about it. Shah had lived in U.K for few years and made Ned realise. It all made sense to Ned about the cautious and discreet approach to the situation. They agreed that it was the actual reason for Kay's preparation for her parents. Shah offered his support to Ned and said that he would be in the club. So after meeting the parents (very briefly) he should come to him to chat as usual. Ned was then upset as he stayed in England all this time and never had any difference made to his actual colour or country of birth. He was concerned and he needed to speak to Kay about it as a matter of urgency. Following the discussion with Shah he went to his room to get ready for the club as usual. He looked at his best as usual and strolled to the club late as usual after his works. He got to the club at 10.30 in the evening. He walked through the door and looked for Kay from the corner of his eyes and went straight to Shah. He got a beer (he did not like beer) for the first time and lit a cigarette from Shah. During this period he kept looking at the situation passively. After a quick sip and a cigarette in between his fingers he went to Kay. "Hello Ned I thought you would not be coming" exclaimed Kay. "You know me, late as usual. I have been quite busy", replied Ned. "Mum, dad, meet Ned, Ned meet my mum and dad", Kay introduced. Her father stood up and shook Ned 's hand and stared at him in his eyes. By then Ned was rather relaxed and could not be bothered about anything. Ned was polite about it all and then Kay's mum stood up and shook his hand. They both said that they heard a lot about him and Ned smiled to this comment as he did not know how to behave anymore. Standing next to her parents he finished his beer and offered to buy everyone a drink. Kay and her parents refused and Ned excused himself and went to get another beer for himself. He was not a beer drinker and was getting drunk quickly. Kay was constantly checking her parents and to whom they were talking to just in case they came across someone who was not aware of the situation. Ned went to Shah and remained there for the rest of the evening. Kay came to Ned for a chat and asked him what he thought of her parents. His reply was "very polite and caring but I do not think they like foreigners! Do they, Kay?". Kay did not say anything to this comment and offered Ned another drink. She looked at Shah and suggestively asked him to take care of Ned. Shah understood the situation and kept Ned by his side. He felt strongly for both of them, and again who would understand them better than himself. "I have been there before Kay. Do not worry everything will be okay. I would advise you to speak to Ned as soon as you can" Shah requested.

While Kay was talking to Shah, her parents were talking to Jane who accidentally told them that Kay and Ned were the best of friends in the nurse's home. 'Best of friends!', Kay's parents knew very well that adults could only be good friends for one reason. After Jane left their company, Kay's dad asked his wife whether Kay knew what she was doing being a good friend to someone strange! They looked at each other worryingly and looked at Kay talking to Ned and Shah. They were good friends but their body language was saying something totally different. Anyhow they thought that may be, just may be they are good friends, and decided not to ask Kay anything about it. Kay went back to them with a big smile on her face and asked her parents what they thought of her friends. Their comments were that they were fine but they were concerned about Ned's alcoholic behaviour and his chain smoking. Kay was quick in defending him and said that he was a bit stressed and tired but he was really a gentleman and very helpful. However her parents made it clear they did not like his drinking and smoking but again he was just a friend and they were not that bothered. They spoke with double meaning when they talked about Ned. Neither party was ready to speak about this subject openly. Before leaving the club Kay went to say good-bye to Ned and Shah and promised to see them when her parents had gone. Kay's parents said goodnight to them and they left the club. They went to their room and they retired as they all had a busy day. In the club Shah and Ned were drunk and had to be carried back to their room by other club members. They collapsed in their room and stayed there the rest of the following day. They did not see Kay's parents again.

In the morning, Kay and her parents went for their breakfast in the canteen and they met Kay's friends. They had a good chat about various things and life in the nurses' home in general. Kay's parents were satisfied that their daughter was content and comfortable. They liked her friends. Although they did not quite like Kay's association with Ned yet they did not make any further comment about it. Afterwards they went to central London for shopping to Harrods and visit few other places of interest. They all got back late in the afternoon. Her mum and dad got ready to go home. Kay was sad to see them go as she missed her parents very much. There were tears of sadness on both sides and her parents departed. Kay was pleased about their visit but she was getting desperate to see Ned. As soon as they waved goodbye, Kay went straight to Ned's room. She knocked at the door but there was no answer although the music was on. She knocked few times and then left a message on the notepad on the door.

Meanwhile Ned was at Shah's. They were catching up from the previous night. Ned did not know what to think of Kay's parents and decided that he would carry on as normal and that he would make the most of the time he could for as long as he was with Kay. He really loved Kay and was not going to do anything to lose her. Shah advised him to take it easy and let things move as they go and deal with it as the issue arise. Shah said "better be happy for the two days that to be unhappy for the rest of your life". To that Ned left and went to his room. There he saw Kay's note. He did not go in, instead he went to Kay. He knocked and the door was answered straight away. Ned did not have time to step in that Kay jumped on him and gave a good hug and a kiss. "I missed you, darling. I missed touching you, missed kissing you, missed seeing you late at night", said Kay. "I missed you too", replied Ned. They kissed each other passionately and ended up in bed. They had wild sex and just would not stop. After a good two-hour of lovemaking they finally settled down with a cup of tea. They were both holding each other in bed as if they had been apart for years. It was only a day, a night and a day. They were quiet for a while and then Ned asked Kay what her parents thought about him. "They were pleased seeing my friends and they were very relieved that you help me and all sorts", Kay replied. Ned was not convinced and told her that he felt that they were not convincing in that they liked him as her friend. Kay tried to convince Ned but was not successful and burst out in tears. "I am sorry Ned. I knew my parents would not approve of you that was why I was very careful about anything I said. You know it has been stressful. I love my parents and I did not want to hurt them", Kay replied. Ned looked at her and looked deep into her eyes and was trying to understand her and said, "well, I can say that your parents do not like your association with me because I am a foreigner; whether you like it or not Kay, my feelings cannot be wrong". Kay held Ned even closer and more tightly and sobbed. "It is okay you know. I understand now why you had to talk to everyone who would have been involved with them. If that's how you want it then I do not mind. You are here now and that's what matters to me at the moment. Tomorrow who knows, it never comes anyway!", Ned commented. Kay cried non-stop and sat down in bed next to Ned and said "I know my parents do not like foreigners but I cannot help having feelings for you!", said Kay. "Well if you knew, then may be you should have thought about it before you went out with me", said Ned. "Look... I like you very much and I am fond of you. I made my bed and now I have to sleep in it", said Kay. Ned asked Kay to tell him more about her parents so that in future if they visit then he would know what to do. He knew Kay would not back down and continued her relationship with Ned. However, Kay told him a lot about their views and feelings about immigrants. From childhood they were warned about mixing with people from different countries and different races. But Kay could not help it. She enjoyed eating the forbidden apple and as the taste got better she kept at it. To sum it up Kay told Ned one line that they, her sister and herself, have been reminded of throughout their childhood and adulthood, 'all men are equal until they walk through our driveway'. Ned thanked Kay for telling him these and they stayed in bed until late in the evening.

14

They were there physically and somewhere else spiritually. Kay was thinking about her future without Ned and how difficult it would be to get used to going out and sleeping with white men again. To her it was different ways of living, talking, having sex and thinking compared to the standard boring ways she knew. For Kay, going out with Ned was a spicy way to live, always full of surprises and never a dull moment. She was thinking about the changes she would have to put up with when it was over with Ned but she was determined to make it last for as long as possible as she knew deep down that she could not go anywhere near the subject of 'marriage'. Whereas Ned's thoughts were different. Ned was in love with Kay and was not even thinking about what he would feel like to be with someone else when it would be over with Kay. In fact, the end of his relationship with Kay never even crossed his mind. He was thinking about ways he could adopt to convince Kay's parents about accepting people from different culture and race, indifferent of colour. Ned knew that colour was the biggest issue although Kay did not make it that clear to him. As in the past Kay had a boyfriend who was from a rich Greek family and was adored by her parents because he was white and of course was rich. They were in fact looking into and perhaps Kay's reconciliation with the Greek boyfriend so that there would be a possible engagement and may be a wedding. With that bit of important information Ned knew exactly what the problem was. He was not black but fair and handsome enough for all the girls to run after him. However, from that day Ned psychologically conditioned himself and he was always ready for the unexpected. He was always ready for disappointment, but for him what mattered was that he loved Kay and knew that Kay loved him too (or at least she said so many times).

After resting with Kay and having a good think of the situation he went to his room and continued with his work. Ned was restless in bed that night. He could not find peace and was constantly thinking. He got up at 5 in the morning and got ready for college and from then onwards listened to some Indian love music until it was time for breakfast. He went to the canteen and waited for Kay. They met and after breakfast Ned decided to tell Kay of his decision. "Kay, I love you very much, you know that. But having had a good think about the whole situation I have come to the conclusion that we should split up in order to avoid further hurt and distress to you and myself" said Ned to Kay. Kay looked at him in the eyes. She could tell that Ned has not slept all night as his eyes were red and swollen which was unlike him. She looked at him continuously and was trying to understand the situation that she knew clearly, and there was no one better placed than Kay to know what was expected in the future. Yet she burst in tears and walked away. In the coach they sat separately. Although very sad they did not say a word to anyone and continued with their day as if there was nothing unusual. They got back in the evening. At night Kay's slot in the schedule was empty as she was not there, and they were both feeling empty and they were both missing each other. Ned was determined not to go to see Kay and with his discipline he was sticking by it. Whereas Kay, although she knew that there was a lot of emotional turmoil expected yet she was ready to stick with Ned for as long as she could and make the most of the time she had with him. So as she did not see any reaction from Ned, she decided to go and clear the air.

She knocked at Ned's door. Once, twice, and three times, there was no reply. She knew Ned would be in, so she pushed the door and let herself in. In her mind she had to be with him. So she got in and took herself to Ned's bed and sat next to him. "Darling I know what you mean but don't you think that it is useless to make such decisions at this time?", asked Kay. Ned had no reply, as anything he would say would be no good, as he loved her. While Kay did not get a reply, she leaned on Ned and kissed him. Ned did not speak a word for the entire evening and Kay seduced him like never before and they had wonderful sex with passion. Kay had the best orgasm of her life. She came twice in a matter of minutes. After sex she held Ned on top of her and cried. "I love you so much. I do not know what there is in the future but I want to be with you, I know that", said Kay. She held Ned tighter to her and cried for a long time. Ned was quiet. He held her tight to reassure her but did not know what to do anymore. All he knew was that he loved her ... and ... he loved her ... and ... would always love her. He was not confused but did not know how to deal with this situation. He never had such experience before where he had to deal with mixed race relationship although they were of the same religion. He just let himself go and made his mind that he would carry on as if there was no issues and that he would take a risk. If it would work out then great and if it did not then he had to face up with the consequences. He was strong and he knew that if it went to pieces then he would have to let go of Kay no matter how much he loved her and no matter how much it hurt. He did not say a word to Kay regarding this issue and fell asleep. Kay left late from Ned's room. She left a note on the table reading:

"Dear love,
Thank you for a magnificent evening and thank you for being with me. You are the best thing that ever happened to me. I am fond of you and will always love you. See you for breakfast tomorrow.
                Love you.
                Kay."

They did not stay away from each other and as usual they could not keep their hands off each other. Sex every night and day, sometimes three times a day but definitely every day. They were both healthy and attractive so they never got bored as they tried out their various fantasies and anything they could think of to make sex wild with passion. Any time anyone would visit Ned or Kay they would be either naked or they would be in their dressing gown. They were well-known and were the desire of the nurse's home. Most girls wanted and would do anything to have Ned for one night and the same with Kay and men. However, then onwards things went very well except when college holidays approached and they started missing each other

15

Summer holiday came quick and Kay and Ned knew what the situation would be like. So Ned decided to buy a car so that he would be able to drop Kay at home and pick her up and also do sneak visits for sex in the wild. But what car? He had to buy something he could afford, maintain and manage financially. That was a real issue for him as he did not make any such commitments as buying a car in England. So he had to do some homework on it and had Kay to help him on that venture.

Ned and Kay bought a variety of newspapers and magazines to look for the appropriate car that would fit the budget. They looked hard and could not find a car that could be managed on Ned's monthly allowance. And Ned was not in the habit of doing joint business for the fear that everything might turn ape-shape. So they looked for a good while until Ned decided that he would get a cheap car – a banger as Kay called it. Kay was not bothered what car as it was not hers and all she wanted was for Ned to visit her. So Ned located a small two door Honda Civic. The car was older than him by one year. Ned went to see it and looked around, inside and outside although he did not know what he was looking for. He pretended that he knew and asked few questions that were totally irrelevant as the car was visibly old as specified in the newspaper. The owner of the car was an old man, he did not answer any questions of Ned and just stood there looked at what Ned was looking at. The price was £300.00 for a small old car. But again better cars were in the range of thousands of pounds. So he tried to haggle with the owner. It was no good; the owner would not change his mind. "Three hundred pounds. Take or leave it," said the owner. Ned looked around and offered £250.00. The owner was not to budge. He took the car key off Ned's hand and was locking the doors. He was starting to walk away when Ned gained his attention with his demand of £300.00. The car drove well, at least when Ned saw it and he was pleased with it. He got in his car and drove to the nurse's home. Seeing Ned driving in the car park Kay came running to him. She liked the car although it was very old and unattractive. "It is a sweet car, darling. Stay here I will get my camera and take a picture of your first car" said Kay. She ran to her room and came back with her camera and took few pictures of Ned posing on his newly acquired property. They both planned a night out driving the car to the river for a beautiful romantic evening. Ned parked the car, looked at it and felt proud of his achievement – owning a car. They both went to their rooms and Ned called his parents and told them the story about the car. Of course where he came from owning a car was 'the thing', that is, one had to be rich. His parents and brothers and sisters were over the moon. He promised to send them a picture of it in the near future. Furthermore, Kay called her parents and told them that Ned had bought a car and that he offered her a lift when she would go home for her summer holiday. Her parents did not mind as that generosity of Ned saved them money, time and inconvenience altogether. After having a good chat with her parents, Kay went to Ned and told him about the chat with her parents and that it was okay for him to take her home. At least that was a positive step, again 'until they walk through our driveway'. Ned had to be reassured by Kay that he wouldn't be treated like a driver, unloading her luggage and be turned away from the driveway. Kay was upset by this comment and wished she did not tell him anything about her parents' views. Ned apologised and they started planning for their evening out in the new/old car. Kay prepared a little picnic they would have on the riverbank late that night. Kay had a small bottle of champagne to celebrate the occasion. Very exceptional indeed as she always tried to make Ned smile. They set off from the nurse's home and after half an hour in the small lanes of the countryside they reached the river. There were a lot of barges and small boats. The place was busy and they felt secure. They located a private spot where they would not be spotted by walkers and set their picnic. They lay down on the blanket they brought from the nurses home and looked at the sky and the stars. They enjoyed their champagne, sandwiches, crisps and cheesecake. It was a romantic evening. They kissed and cuddled and when it got late they embarked in an open-air sex session. After sex Ned could not help himself from laughing. It reminded him of his camping trip with Shah. He told Kay about it and it became a private joke since then – squeaking in the middle of the night. They had a beautiful evening and packed up and went to the car.

They got in and Ned tried to start the car. No luck. He tried again and again and again. The beautiful night was taking the wrong turn. He opened the bonnet and checked the leads and got underneath the car and saw nothing unusual. He got in and tried again. The car was dead. He was disappointed. Kay was very diplomatic, and was saying nothing, as at that moment saying anything at all would be the wrong thing. So she reassured Ned that it would be okay and that she would call her parents and used their AA car recovery card to get them back to the nurse's home. There was no other choice, so they were walking towards the phone box, when they saw James from the nurses home driving past them. They stopped him and asked for help. James was a very kind and generous person and came to their rescue. He took his jump lead out and restarted Ned's car. James looked at Ned's car and could say nothing but "well ... it is a good car... it just needs some looking after". He escorted Ned and Kay up to the nurse's home just in case they got stuck again. After that they went their separate ways to their rooms. Ned and Kay enjoyed the evening and said good night in the car park. Kay was content with the evening as after all the car was not her problem. She met her friends in her corridor and told them about their lovely romantic evening out, and about the car breaking down. Just as well it was only the battery so they comforted each other that it would be okay. For Ned, it was a disappointment that cost him £300.00. If the car broke down after a week he would not be bothered but on the first day, that was unacceptable.

Somehow, his enthusiasm about he car wore out on the same night and he had a bad feeling about it altogether.

The next day he went to have the car insured. He went to the brokers and got few quotes. First quote £900.00, then £1500.00, then £700.00, and then he gave up. He came back home and spoke to Kay about it and expressed his disbelief. The insurance was a lot more than the car was worth. He was angry as everything was falling apart, the car breaking down and then the expensive insurance. Kay offered her support and mentioned her dad's friend who was a broker and would look for a cheaper option. She called her dad and asked him if he could help Ned with an affordable insurance. Her dad obliged but at the same her dad was noticing Kay's help to Ned. He did not say anything to her daughter and would not refuse her anything. So he gave Kay the telephone number of Jack. She called Jack and explained the situation and she got the cheapest insurance quote of £350.00 on third party, fire and theft. That was the best they could get. To pay that sum at once having just bought the car was impossible, so Kay negotiated a payment plan of three months with Jack. All done, Ned thanked Kay and her father for their help. He got the insurance papers within days. Ned did not drive the car for three days whilst waiting for the insurance papers. He cleaned the car and polished it. He added few decorations and the car looked real cool. The car was a highlight and it was a luxury as a student nurse to own a car. He introduced the car to Shah and others he knew in the nurse's home.

After receiving all the relevant papers for the car, he took the car for a spin. He went about a mile and the car just died. "Not again" he screamed. He got out of the car in the middle of the road, holding the traffic behind. He tried to push it on the pavement but it was too heavy for him to push alone. Two men came out from their car behind him and helped him push it on the pavement and they left. Ned was there, all embarrassed and ready to die at the time. It was just unbelievable. He did the same thing, looked around and could not find anything wrong. He went to the house where he parked and asked for help. An old man came and helped him with the car and suggested that he had the car checked for battery and alternator. He thanked the old man and drove back to the nurse's home. He knew what the battery was but not the alternator. So on the way he bought a new battery for his car, had it fitted and drove the car around for a while. The car sounded well and healthy and did not breakdown. He was pleased and felt better. He went back home and parked the car. Kay came to see him afterwards and they decided to go for a late night drive to relax and cool themselves from the stress from the studies. They got in the car and drove about two hundred metres and the car stopped. This time they pushed the car back to the car park and left it until the next morning. All of Ned's time and patience was taken up by this old car. From then onwards Ned pushed the car more than he drove it for about two weeks. Kay could not bear the unhappiness shadowing Ned so she called her dad for support. Then she went to Ned and told him about having to change the alternator. The next day Ned got a quote of £75.00 to have a reconditioned one fitted in. He agreed to it straight away as he was in no mood. The alternator fitted, the car was driving perfectly well and since then they went out and about without the fear of getting stuck. They finally settled down after two weeks of running after the car and pushing it. Just as well as it was time that Kay went home for summer.

The night before taking Kay to her home they had a long talk about how they were going to meet in the middle of the holidays. Kay drew a map of where to meet her and where they were going to spend the evening so that they would not be seen by friends and families. Kay felt horrible as she was happy with Ned yet she did not feel free due to the circumstances. Kay also spoke to Ned about expected behaviour at her home and warned about getting in deep discussion with her mum. They would behave as friends and not couples. Ned had no choice but to accept. They talked about their relationship and saw that there was no future because of the parents' situation and they were both saddened by it. However, they decided to continue despite the bleak future. Whilst talking they drunk a bottle of wine and spent quality time together and slept in the same bed. It was a single bed and uncomfortable to sleep together but they were missing each other so much they put up with the discomfort and spent as much time together as possible.

16

The next morning they got up early and packed up the car. Ned checked the car all over to make sure he could make the return journey safely. He topped the oil, water and checked the brakes oil. All checks were completed quickly. They started their longest trip in the car. They drove up the motorway without any problems. The car sounded supreme and healthy. Ned made a rest stop at the services on the motorway to fill the car up with petrol. Although he was shocked with the sky-high cost of unleaded petrol, he had no choice but to buy it. Afterwards, they went to the shops and bought few things and they had lunch. Kay offered to buy the lunch as Ned made the effort to drive her home. They enjoyed the expensive lunch and continued their trip. After four hours (which would normally take two hours) drive Ned reached the village where Kay lived. He stopped the car and was reviewing his decision. He was not sure whether he was bold enough to face her parents in her house. Ned was sweating a lot and was feeling vulnerable as he already knew their feelings about foreigners. Kay reassured him that she would be by him all the time to avoid any such discussion. Kay knew Ned well enough not to allow her parents to raise any such conversations as Ned was not the type to sit and take it all, he was rather polite and could answer very well with sarcasm. Kay was in the middle of all this and was determined to bring Ned home. After few minutes of rest and when Ned calmed down they drove to Kay's house. Kay instructed Ned to park his car in the driveway same as everyone else. So Ned did as he was asked. Kay's parents were waiting patiently as they were worried about Kay's safety with Ned's first ever trip on the motorway. However, as they got in the driveway, Kay's parents came running with excitement and kissed and hugged while Ned unloaded the car. He felt like a mini-cab driver for a while. Kay was still greeting her mum when her dad came to Ned and first things he asked was to park the car on the road, in order to leave the driveway free. Ned did not reply and started the car. Kay looked back and gave a dirty look to her dad but made no comments. Ned's look to Kay and his expression on his face was enough. While driving the car out Ned expertly spun the wheels so that all the gravels would scatter everywhere and so it did. He was pleased when he saw Kay's father's expression on his face. He parked the car on the road and stayed there as if waiting for Kay's good-bye. Kay came running to him and said "you are not going back, are you? You have to come inside for a cup of tea at least". Ned was not sure about all this on the first trip. So he whispered to Kay, "are you sure of what you are asking me? So far I am only out of the driveway. I do not want to be ridiculed, so may be I should make a move". "Oh no! Oh no! You will only go over my dead body. Please come with me", Kay whispered back. Meanwhile her parents were watching them and their intimacy with disapproval. So Ned proudly got out of the car and walked next to Kay to her parents. Kay introduced Ned again and there were greeting from both sides. One could tell looking at the scene that the parents were not at all pleased, especially having neighbours from both sides peeping out of their windows. No black men have ever come to their road let alone walking in their house with their daughter. To them it was a disgrace and not good for their reputation. Before they could actually walk into their house one of the neighbours came out and respectfully greeted Ned (better than Kay's parents) and welcomed him to England and to the North. She asked Ned few nosy questions and invited Ned for a cup of tea should he have some time or on his next visit. Ned was not pleased about it as he knew that the neighbours were close and over-protective of each other. So that would be another way for her parents to find out more about them. He politely declined the offer for the day but promised that he would certainly visit the next time for tea. They got in the house. Ned was standing and was waiting to be seated. He was asked for tea by Kay while her parents were watching every of his move. He was standing until Kay brought the tea. Kay offered him to sit on the single sofa. As soon as Ned sat down, her mother told Kay, "that seat is for the cat my dear, do not forget!". Kay looked at her mum and smiled, "of course mum, how could I forget. May be I will have tea with Ned in the garden". Kay's mum disapproved and accepted that it was all right for Ned to sit there. It was not because he would go in the garden but just in case the neighbours would see him conversing with their daughter. They were all sitting in the lounge with no conversation. Suddenly Kay's mum asked the most awkward questions "if there was to be war, would you go to your country to fight the war?". Very weird, direct and dry question! Ned had to answer, "of course I would. Being in England does not make me English!". Kay knew the bomb would explode and intervened in the conversation. She started talking about the course and all the help Ned provided her with and they talked about the standard joke about the tea and dinner. There was nothing to laugh about no matter how hard Kay tried. After an hour and few cups of tea, Ned left and went to his car for the drive home. Kay came with him and her parents followed behind just to make sure there was nothing going on. They were watching their every move. Ned got in the car, and Kay bent over and gave a kiss on the cheek and said good-bye. She was standing and waiting to wave. Ned started the car, no luck. Tried again, no luck. He got out and looked here there and everywhere and could not work it out. Then he checked again and there was hardly any oil. Kay's father ran to his garage at the back of their garden and brought a new gallon of oil. He offered Ned to use it. Ned used the required amount and gave the rest back, but her father refused and asked Ned to keep it for the rest of the journey. Very unusual, was it to get rid of him quickly or was it genuine generosity? Ned was getting confused. He did not want to waste his time thinking about it as everyone was waiting for him to make a move. He started the car successfully and drove off. Kay waved at him until she could not see him.

Ned gone, Kay got in with her parents and they sat down in the lounge. They shared their experiences without each other and expressed their emotions and missing each other. However, Kay was not in the mood to forget Ned's unwelcomed approach from her parents. She started, " mum, you did not have to be openly horrible to my friend. He drove me all the way from the hospital and I felt like you wanted him out, lets not forget about letting him in. I am quite disappointed". Kay's mum did not waste time in her reply, "how dare you talk to me like that? It is our house and we have the choice of whom we want to allow in the house. Subject close, and do remember that we do not like your company and friendship with him". Kay got very upset and started crying. Her dad could never see her crying and reassured her that they will try to be polite next time and that they will be more welcoming. He also emphasised that they hoped there was nothing further to this friendship and that they would not be pleased to learn that there was a relationship. Kay got the message loud and clear. The subject ended there and they settled down in their usual family life. Nothing was said about the visit since. Kay spoke to Ned on the phone in the night as they missed each other very much. Ned was in the nurse's home and was doing some advanced work with his assignment and as usual went to club and went out with Shah. Days went by and Ned did not forget that he had to visit Kay in the middle of their time apart. Kay never forgot her parents' message but was not giving up the idea of meeting Ned again near her home. Kay had everything planned carefully and they would spend their time away so that no one would even get a hint of what was going on.

The night before Ned's trip to Kay's house they spoke on the phone and planned to meet far away from Kay's parents. Kay gave Ned all the directions and where to meet. The next morning Ned got up early and drove to meet Kay. It was a long drive and without car radio it was difficult to put up with it. The desperation to meet Kay was no competition to any other things even boredom. He reached the meeting point which was a Mac Donald. Kay was impatiently waiting for him there. The moment she saw his little car driving in the car park, she ran to him and gave him a big kiss. They did not waste time in the car park just in case someone saw them. They drove off to the woods nearby. Kay had prepared for a pic-nic. They found a nice and quiet spot and had an enjoyable snack. They talked for hours without realising that time was going too fast. They also had a bottle of wine and ended up having each other in the woods. It was exciting for both of them, risking everything in the middle of nowhere. Of course the place was known to Kay that's why she chose it at first place. They had the most beautiful and romantic time they ever had in the open air. Every time, every hour and every minute they spent was better than the one before. They never got bored of each other. Afterwards they went for a walk in the woods, hand in hand, and occasionally, stopping by to kiss and hug. They valued every second they were together. They walked for over a mile when they suddenly realised that it was getting dark. Kay got worried as Ned was merry but not drunk. She was worried about his journey back. So she had to plan something quickly. They packed up and went to a phone box. Kay called her parents and said that she was meeting Ned in town as he was on his way back from camping. From previous experience of Kay's reaction of receiving Ned, her mum asked her to bring him home for dinner. That was a surprise as Kay was only thinking about spending some more time with Ned until he was sober enough to drive. Anyhow she jumped at this generous offer. So, they went to the shop and Ned bought a bottle of wine for her parents to have at dinner. Then they drove to her house. This time Kay's father waited for them on the road. When he saw Ned's car coming he took his car out of the driveway and offered him to park in his space. That was a shock to both Kay and Ned. So Ned parked his car and received a warm welcome from Kay's parents. They got in the house and Ned had the choice to sit wherever he wanted. No sarcastic comments were made from either side. Kay's father joined Ned in a discussion about sports and latest news on television. They talked sensibly while Kay and her mum were setting the table for dinner. After few minutes Kay's sister arrived from work with her boyfriend. They all joined in a casual talk, joking and laughing. Ned told them where he came from and a little bit about his family overseas. They were impressed with Ned's achievement. Kay's mum commented that they would not entertain any foreigner unless he was of a sporty nature and had good moneymaking potential, but Kay's friend was an exception. To this comment Kay called everyone at the table for dinner. That was expertly timed as Ned was ready for an argument. However, that did not end there. Her mum innocently mentioned about her famous politician, one very well-known for his speech about immigrants. She thought Ned would be ignorant of 1960's politics. He knew exactly what was about to happen. Kay did not know anything about the indirect conversation that was going on but her dad went mute. Her dad was trying to pacify the situation from last time. He hoped that Ned would not know anything about it. Little did they know about Ned so he replied, "funny you said that. Kay do you know about the speeches and policies of one of your local MP?". Kay innocently said no and continued to eat her meal. "Well, may be your mother would like to tell you more about it sometimes!" said Ned. Kay's father was mute with shock. He did not know where to look and what to say. Kay's mum interfered and said, "you seem to be well aware of British politics. It is interesting as many would not even know his name". "You would be surprised as to what I know being in this country for such a short time. I would like to recite the exact words used in one of his best speeches, but I would like to save some indigestion", replied Ned. Kay was still unaware of what was going on. "You seem to have an unknown depth, Ned" said Kay's mum to Ned. "Well, the meal is exquisite, try the wine", said Ned to Kay's mum. "I can see you have a remarkable taste of wine as well!", said her mum. Then finally Kay's dad butted in with his usual sport discussion and her sister's boyfriend joined in. For the rest of the meal Kay's mother had her mouth shut in shame and Ned was quite pleased with that. They both knew what they talked about and her dad of course kept quiet as he would not like Kay to get upset again. They all enjoyed the meal and the wine. It was late by then. So he excused himself to get ready for his journey back. Kay's father was embarrassed about the discussion over dinner. So, he said to Ned that it was late for him to travel back, and in his car it would be risky just in case he broke down. So, he offered Ned to stay the night. To this suggestion, Kay was pleased and shocked as well but her mum was disgusted.

Staying the night did not sound like a good idea to Ned. So he declined the offer as he knew the next morning would bring some more discussion about racism with Kay's mum. Kay looked at Ned and disapproved of his driving under the influence of alcohol. He maintained that he was fine until her mum interfered. She had no choice but to ask Ned to stay, as everyone in the family wanted him to stay. To her request Ned agreed and then the discussion about sleeping arrangement at night started. Her mum offered Ned to take the settee in the lounge, Kay wanted Ned to have her room for the night and her father offered him to stay in the spare room that was meant for visitors. So there they were arguing about it until Ned suggested that he would be better off driving home after few coffees as he did not want to hear any further disagreement. Kay's father asked Kay to make a final decision, as Ned was her friend. So she stuck to her offer of her room. So it was. All agreed and then she went upstairs to set the room for Ned. Downstairs, her parents and Ned continued chatting about his country of birth and schooling. During their friendly chats Ned told them that he was a registered athlete where he came from and that he wanted to pursue his sportive interest. They were quite interested in his sports activities and encouraged him to pursue it in England, as there was good potential to make money and become rich quickly. Ned heard that from them before and decided to discontinue the dialogue otherwise it would lead to other racist comments. Just at that time Kay came down and offered to show Ned the room he would be sleeping in. Ned asked for the permission to go upstairs. Kay introduced him to their bathroom and told him about the different times every member of the family got up so that there would not be any traffic in the corridor in the morning. Then she showed him the room. As soon as they got in she started kissing him and expressed her happiness to his decision for staying. Ned was not sure whether it was a good idea but nevertheless he stayed. Kay also showed him the spare room she would be sleeping in. It was next door, how convenient. They came downstairs, very innocent. As Ned was staying they opened another bottle of wine and continued talking about his homeland. He told them a great deal about it. Kay listened enviously and commented that she would love to visit one day. Ned did not waste time in offering her to visit and stay with him at his parents. He also emphasised that she would have no expenses except for her travel ticket. Kay jumped to this offer as it would be a life time holiday. Staying in a hotel and touring at one's own expense would be a dream. She said she would love it. Her parents were shocked by her reply. They started making a lot of excuses about going to his parents and mixing in different culture. They were not pleased with the idea. But Kay was so excited that they could not discourage her any longer as the conversation was starting to get into an argument. So they agreed that it would be a good idea to think about for the summer holidays. After a long chat Kay's parents went to bed.

Ned and Kay could not wait for them to be asleep than they started cuddling and kissing each other. Every now and then Kay peeped upstairs to see if her parents were fast asleep. They were taking the risk and started having sex in the lounge. It was very inconvenient and uncomfortable due to the high risk involved. They were fully dressed and having the best time of their life. Kay was excited due to the fact that she was having Ned right below her parents' bedroom. There were no noise, no moaning and groaning compared to the usual session. Kay had the greatest orgasm ever before that she burst in tears afterwards. They had a good half an hour of being quiet that they heard a bang on the ceiling. Kay knew it was her father signalling her that it was high time for bed. She never had heard this sound before. So she went upstairs to confirm. As she went upstairs she heard her mum calling her to get to bed as soon as she could make it. She knew they were unhappy about the length of time she spent with Ned downstairs, especially without any voices. Surely they were not asleep all that time. She got worried and hoped that they did not hear a thing. However, she came down and they had another drink and then they went to bed separately. As soon as it was dark everywhere, and Kay could hear her parents snoring, she sneaked into Ned's room (or her room rather). She cuddled him until they were really tired and then she went to her bed. She really enjoyed the time they stayed lying down in her bed. That was the first time she had ever done anything like this. She felt happy and was sure she was in love. She said nothing, as she did not want to give herself hope for anything in the future.

The next morning, as planned they all got up in turn. Ned was the last to get up and use the bathroom. He rolled himself in a towel and went in, had his wash and when getting out, he bumped into Kay's sister. She had never seen a coloured body in real life before (except in movies of course). She stopped and stared at Ned's slim and perfect body. She said nothing and went down. Ned got in the room and was getting ready. Meanwhile, Kay's sister went and told Kay about it in the presence of her mum. She was excited to the fact that Ned looked good. Kay was laughing and said nothing. Her mum stopped her and said, ''you better tell him that he is a guest in the house and I will certainly not tolerate such appearance and behaviour in this house''. Kay could not stop laughing and went upstairs giggling. She told Ned what had happened and asked him to be more careful. So they both went down and Ned apologised about his appearance and they all sat down for breakfast. Nothing un-towards were said. Ned finished his breakfast and bid goodbye and paid compliments to the welcome and hospitality he received for the night. He went out with Kay and when he started driving Kay bent over and kissed him on the lips. Little did she realise that her mum was watching from behind the curtains. Her father was told about it and both parents decided not to tell her anything just in case she left them for Ned. From that time onwards her parents showed her much more love and affection than before. They decided that in order to keep things running smooth and in peace they opted not to ask her if she was seeing Ned. They would ignore the subject and then Kay would hopefully keep it as a friendship relationship to them thus never to have the opportunity to ask anything about a serious relationship with regards to Ned. Nothing horrible about Ned was ever spoken and she spoke to Ned as usual on the phone pretending there was nothing of a relationship until she finished her holidays.

Holidays finished, Ned went to fetch Kay from home. This time everyone's behaviour was different towards him. There were no sarcastic and racist comments made. Ned was welcomed in the house as Kay's best friend and entertained as any other visitors. He was in Kay's house after lunch and picked her up. Her parents and sister came out to the car and bid good-bye. They kissed her and asked her to be careful and be good as usual. Her sister came around and gave her a meaningful long hug and whispered, "I will still love you as my sister no matter what you do. Ned is very handsome and attractive. Mum and dad do not like you getting involved with him but remember no matter what happens in life in the future, I am still your sister and will always love you", in her ear. Ned's hearing was very fine and he got every word of what was said. So he knew that the parents suspected their relationship, hence the pleasant reception at this time. He drove off. Kay and Ned had a long chat about what they did in their times apart on their journey back. They also discussed what her sister said in her whisper. They were not worried about anything anymore and decided that they would talk openly about their relationship to their parents. They caught up with each other. Half way they stopped on the motorway for a snack. Kay opted to pay as Ned was driving. They had a snack and drove back to the nurse's home.

17

Their return together was rather weary for others in the nurse's home. People around did not like that Ned and Kay's relationship was lasting a long time, and that they were continuously in high spirits. After refreshing themselves they met in the club for a drink and meeting colleagues and friends to catch up with holidays and all. Ned was talking to Shah as usual before he went to Kay. And Kay was busy with her friends. However, Jonathan from the club came to Ned and Shah to chat with them as per usual. However, this time he especially came to tell them that he did not like the mixed relationship of Ned and Kay. That started an argument. Shah calmly asked him to move away before there was a fight. He stuck for Ned whilst Ned was getting hot with temper. Minutes after there was a row. Ned said to Jonathan, ''if you were good enough then may be, just may be, you could get a woman or may be keep one of your kind. But you know what, not only that I am better than you but I could also take your wife out if you were married. Thank your star you are not otherwise she would be shagging me. So, here you are, take your chance with my girl. If she takes you, then I will happily back down''. Everyone could hear what Ned said and they were all watching. Jonathan had always been known to be openly racist but never had any such outburst. Jonathan did not know what to say and where to look and suddenly he turned around to Kay and said, "you are a flipping prostitute", and went out of the club. Shah could not control himself and ran after him, Ned followed. There was a fight. Everyone was involved with separating Ned, Shah and Jonathan. There was broken nose and blood around but it was not Ned's and Shah's. Jonathan was banned from the club straight away. Kay was in tears and commented that, "when a white man goes out with black woman or girl, they say that he scored, and when a white girl goes out with a black man, then she is called a prostitute, how nice, charming". She never experienced such disgrace in her life and did not know what to do. So, she ran out of the club crying. Ned tried to go after her but her friends stopped him and they went to comfort her instead. The night ended in big arguments in the club because of the fighting. Ned and Shah ended up leaving the club early to avoid another fight. The good thing was that they found that their so-called friends in the club were really no friends but people full of pretence. They were in fact xenophobic and the only one who had the gut to say anything was Jonathan. They were disgusted and went back to Kay's rooms to see how she was. They stayed there for a while until she was calm and then they left for their rooms. From that day onwards they knew how to behave with the others in the club.

Since then Ned and Shah only spoke to each other in the club and Kay went to the club rarely. Meanwhile both Kay and Ned had a lot of homework to do for their course and were seen together very little. For them it was not a problem as they knew they had to get on with their studies in order to have a career. Ned would be with Shah most of the time. The next holiday came too soon. Ned remembered that he offered Kay to come to his homeland. So there was a lot of planning to do. He touched on this subject again to check if Kay still wanted to come with him. Kay was not ready to back off. Instead she really wanted to meet Ned's parents and that would help her understand Ned very well. At the same time she would experience life in a different culture and country, an experience she never had before. On their family holidays they always stayed in hotels and enjoyed the beach and organised tours. For her going with Ned would be a life-time experience. Ned wanted to be sure so that he would not be disappointed should she change her mind as he had to notify his parents overseas and of course that would involve certain preparations to receive Kay. Ned was delighted that Kay was going and he called his parents and let them know about her visit. The plan would be that Ned would go the week before and meet all his friends and relatives and then when Kay would come they would go out visiting and touring and live at home. That way she would not be overwhelmed with hundreds of people coming to see Ned. That was decided with Kay and then it was her turn to inform her parents of her decision. She did not want to do it straight away, as she was sure that it would create conflicts and arguments. So she left it for a couple of weeks and continued with her studies and her hospital placements. Time came when Ned had to book his ticket and for Kay to do the same otherwise they would not get a flight that would be convenient for their travel to accommodate college dates. So Kay had no choice but to tell her parents. She called home and her mum picked the phone up. She spoke to her about general and usual issues about college and studies and hospital experience. Her mother did not ask her anything about Ned. After catching up with her mum, she told her that the reason for calling her was to inform her that for the next college holidays she would be going away to visit Ned in his country of birth and also see his family. Her mother was shocked and could not believe it. She could not say a word. Nothing was coming out of her mouth, it all went quiet. Kay was patiently waiting for a comment. At the end of the line, Kay mum beckoned her husband to come to the phone. She handed the phone over to him and sat down on the floor. Kay asked her what was happening but her mum could not reply. Her father answered the phone and asked Kay about the conversation she was having with her mum, which nearly made her collapse. Kay told her dad that she was going with Ned on holidays. After knowing the content of the conversation he asked Kay to come home to discuss her holidays with her parents. Kay knew that the situation was getting worse by the minute and told her dad that she would come over on her next days off. He asked her to come without Ned as they had to talk about it in great depth and details. After the phone call Kay came running to Ned in tears and told him what happened. They were both upset as her mum was in shock with that simple news. So they had a long chat. Kay was determined to go no matter what anyone thought about them but they also agreed to tell her parents that they were only good friends. That hurt Kay very much as she could not share her happiness with her parents and sister and her friends.

After that conversation with Ned, life in the nurse's home was a bit sad for them, as they knew that there was absolutely no future for them together. They decided that they would make the most of the time they had together and if anything improved then they would think about the future but nothing for the time being. One thing that improved throughout their relationship was sex. They were getting more adventurous and explorative. There was never a dull moment alone. They got used to the idea of Kay's parents not accepting the situation. But sex was great so they did not care very much afterwards. In few days they settled down with the situation and Kay had to go home for the weekend to discuss her holidays with Ned. She was confident and as usual she was accompanied by Ned to the train station in central London. They waved each other good-bye. In the train Kay was very upset about the whole thing and was quietly crying her heart out. She was in a dream and wished that things would change for her for the better. Ned went back home from the station and straight to visit Shah and then they went out for a meal and met up with other friends and went out to town for a pub-crawl and afterwards ended up in the dance club.

On the side of England, Kay got home late as she missed her train connection. Her father came to pick her up from the station and as they were tired nothing was spoken on that night. She was welcomed as usual as if there was nothing unusual and had a quick chat with her mum and checked that she was okay. All done she went for a shower and then called Ned in the middle of the night. They spoke for a short time as Ned was drunk and they went to bed. The next morning Kay got up at her parent's and they had breakfast as usual. Kay was waiting for the conversation about her holiday to start but nothing was happening and she was not opting to begin. The morning went by and her mother had been busy cooking and preparing snacks. Kay and her sister were helping. Her dad was cleaning the garden and tidying the lawn. Everyone was busy. Kay did not know what to make of the situation. She was called home to talk things over and so far the issue was being ignored. The conversation was normal as if Ned never existed. She decided to wait. Just before they sat down for lunch, the phone rang. Her sister answered. It was Ned. She called Kay and told her whom the call was from and she went to the lounge and made herself comfortable before Kay started talking on the phone. Ned and Kay spoke for about half an hour about their usual day and most importantly about the talk she was supposed to have at home. She was talking freely to Ned as her sister closed the door behind her after handing her the phone. Nothing was said. Ned said to Kay that the possibilities were that she might have to travel with him as all the seats were booked but that he would keep on looking. Anyhow, no one made any comments about the call or whom it was from. Kay was jolly in her self. At 1.00 in the afternoon, her mother called as it was time for lunch (or should it be dinner). She terminated her call and came to the dining room with all smiles. She was still waiting for someone to say something about her holidays. Instead they were talking about shopping, grandmother and uncles and aunties. Kay did not know what was going on, she did not have the slightest idea. Lunch was great. It was business as usual. They all went and sat in the living room as usual with their cup of tea.

The bell rang. Kay was shocked. No one was expected. Or at least she was not told that anyone was expected. No words were spoken by anyone. Her dad got up and went to open the door. Kay followed behind. Her dad pulled the door open and to Kay's surprise, it was her auntie Margaret. Margaret and Kay got on very well and they shared the same ambition and pleasure. "What a surprise!", screamed Kay. She jumped on to the neck of auntie Margaret and kissed her and hugged her as she had not seen her since she started her nursing course. "It is a pleasure to see you love. You look like a fully fletched woman, not the girl who used to hang on me all the time... very pleased to see you. Are you going to ask me in or what?", said Margaret to Kay. "Now, now, now auntie... come in. We were just having a cup of tea. Come on join us. I will make you a lovely hot one", Kay replied. Her auntie went to the lounge and greeted everyone and she sat down. Kay went to the kitchen and brought her a hot cup of tea. They were talking and catching up about general things. Then after 15 minutes, the bell rang again. Kay was surprised again. She said nothing and stayed in the living room talking to her auntie. Her dad went to answer the door. She heard him talking in his usual tone and she could see someone coming in. "Grandmother!!", she creamed. She jumped up and went over to help her walk to the living room. She kissed and cuddled and hugged. They were a very close family and the excitement of meeting everyone was just brilliant. Her grandmother sat down next to Kay and again they started catching up and talking about general things. Kay was excited that she was not thinking about her holidays or anything else. For her it was great to have the family around just like the old days and having a good old chat. Then another 15 minutes, again the bell rang. Kay said to everyone, "now lets see who is missing to make it complete. Who will have a bet that it will be uncle George?". She took herself to the door happily and to her surprise it was the neighbours. It was excellent for her as she was meeting everyone on a weekend. This had not happened in a long time. As soon as they went to the lounge then the bell rang again. She went for it and this time it was her uncle George, auntie and her two cousins who were about the same age as her. It was kind for everyone to come and they went to gather in the living room, which by then was full. So full that Kay and her sister had to sit on the floor. Everyone had a cup of tea in the hand and then talking and laughing and joking like good old times. Kay totally forgot the reason for her visit home, as she was glad to see everyone. Then her auntie Margaret who was always the most respected and authoritative figure of the family asserted herself to get everyone's attention. "Okay everyone; I am sure everyone knows why we are meeting here today. First of all I have to thank one and all for the effort and time to gather", said Margaret. Kay was not paying attention to anything that was said in the few lines and she was really excited. For Kay it was brilliant that she could meet everyone in one day. "It is with great pleasure that we have seen every nephews and nieces and grandchild growing and it is pleasurable indeed that we are still here and talking today. So in order to keep our little family together we are here to talk about Kay today, isn't that right Kay?" said Margaret. Kay startled at hearing her name and a direct question to her. Surprised and shocked she said "what? I do not know what you mean". "It is about your holiday with Ned", interrupted her mum. Kay was shocked and embarrassed and did not know what to say. She was not aware that her private life was a public meeting or family meeting. Never in her life did she have to attend a family gathering to talk about such things. She was disappointed, especially that she did not know about the family meeting. To her she was meeting everyone as usual and this time it was special for her as she had not met anyone since she started her course. She just did not know what to say. She was frozen and was looking at her mum straight in the eyes. After few seconds she got up and said, "that's interesting…would have been courteous to know at least that there was a family meeting about my holiday. I know we love each other very much and now I know that we really love each other. So if you do not mind I would like to get myself another cup of tea to start with so that I will not have to get up again during this precious meeting – about my holiday. Anyone for a fresh cup of tea?". No one answered. Kay walked to the kitchen and quietly burst into tears. She filled the kettle with water and waited for it to boil. The wait was very long and she was standing there thinking. She felt that she was violated by her own family. She could not share her love for Ned with anyone and then she even had to justify her trip with him. She felt betrayed as no one told her about the so-called meeting. She was sobbing but had to get to grips. She kept wiping the tears off but could not help it. So she splashed water onto her eyes and settled down. She put some face cream that was lying on the windowsill and tried her best to look normal and usual. She made her tea and went to the living room. Meanwhile everyone was quiet in the living room. From the time she left to make tea until she came back nobody said a word as auntie Margaret was in control and of course no one wanted to hurt Kay's feelings just in case she heard anything said about her. She walked in and sat on the floor next to her grandmother.

Margaret started, "so what is this new thing about going on holiday with Ned?". "Auntie, I do not know why there should be a meeting about just a holiday" replied Kay. "I don't think you are getting the point Kay. We all love you and we certainly do not want you to have a hard life simply because we know you better. You are not geared towards living another lifestyle" commented Margaret. "I still do not understand where this is all coming from and going to. Can someone please say what is going on here!", exclaimed Kay. "Kay, darling, I have been a nurse for 26 years and I know what goes on in the nurses' home. We think you are seeing Ned and we are worried that the relationship is getting serious. If there is anything we would rather you let us know", said Margaret. Meanwhile Kay's mother and father were sitting quiet and listening to Kay's answers. No one else was talking except Margaret. Inside, Kay was fuming. She knew she was trapped and had to get herself out of the situation. She already worked out in her mind that she would maintain that Ned was a good friend and so he would always be and no more than that. Her family members were very much against foreigners and there was no point fighting and losing battle with them no matter how much she loved Ned. The second thing in her mind was that she was going on holiday no matter what and nobody was going to stop her.

Kay looked at her auntie and replied assertively, "auntie and everyone else it is important that all of you listen very carefully what I have to say as I am not going to repeat it again whether you like it or not". To that, everyone straightened on his or her seat. What was Kay about to say? Was she going to tell them that she was in love with Ned and that she was going to marry him? Everyone's mind was working at triple speed. They were all eager to know what Kay was about say. Kay continued, "my parents and my sister have met Ned and also entertained Ned, good welcome or awkward one, does not matter. The fact is that you now know Ned. He has been the best man friend I have known in my life. He is a friend and a very good and genuine one too. I know all of you think that I am in love and I know that you are … open-minded … and … not racially prejudiced … by any means but he is my friend and I cannot stress it any more. There is nothing happening. As for the holidays, he has offered me accommodation and he will take me around. What is so bad about that? I cannot go on holiday to his homeland even if I was earning good money. So, for me it is a lifetime's opportunity and I am going whether you like it or not. We have been on many holidays together but what have we learnt? We stayed in a hotel and ate European food, we went touring and befriended European people, we went everywhere with people similar to us, what have we achieved? I want to go there and experience the life that is lived, good experience or bad experience, I want to learn things and go forward in life. Has anyone got any problem with that? I would advise you to voice your opinions and questions now as I am not coming all the way from the nurse's home to justify myself". Everyone was quiet to Kay's speech. They kept thinking. There were no questions and no comments. They were shocked by her speech. They never thought that Kay felt so strongly about her friendship with Ned and about going to his homeland. They said nothing. Kay went to the kitchen and had a drink of water. She was standing there quietly and was in tears but she had to go back and pretend to be strong so that her speech would not be in vain. She felt so lonely and she knew that there would be no support from any member of her family with regards to Ned. She could hear talks in the other room.

Whilst she was in the kitchen the rest of them were talking among themselves. The comments were that they had to hope that Kay was honest. No one believed what Kay just said but they had to listen and the best way to be would be to let her live the way she wanted and hopefully she would see the light. They agreed that they would not ask her anything about Ned and that everyone would treat her with much love so that she would always find it difficult to move with Ned if it were true that they were going out.

After few minutes Kay came back. Aunt Margaret sat upright and said, "Kay darling, we only wanted to talk to you for your own benefit. We love you that's why we care about you. We believe what you have said as we have known you from a little girl. Do as you like with regard to your holiday but if ever there was something happening with Ned we would rather know about it. No matter what happens, or with whom it happens we would always love you. That's all from me. Now if anyone have anything to say, now is your chance".

No one had anything to say except her grandmother, "Kay, I love you dearly and you know that. I will always love you no matter what and wherever you are", said her grandmother holding her hands. That was all that was said. Kay was in a pickle. She did not have enough courage to say anything. Her emotions were bottled up and she was desperate to go back and talk to Ned. But say what to him! She could not tell him what happened, he would never come again. She had to keep the balance on both side and to do that she would have to suffer. One thing for sure was that nobody would ever ask her private questions about Ned. So she would have to play her cool and act accordingly when she would be with her parents and Ned together.

All discussions ended, the whole family stayed back and Kay's mum cooked supper for all. They all enjoyed the rest of the evening after a stressful and tense short discussion. They had lots of wine and whisky and everyone was relaxed and laughing about different issues. The evening went as if nothing happened in the afternoon. Kay was merry but would always remember the afternoon and may be for the rest of her life. She did not hate her parents but hated herself for falling in love with Ned. But again it was not her fault; Ned was a well-mannered, charming, chivalrous and a sex beast full of potential in life ahead. Anyone who would be female would go for him. She just felt lucky to have him and unlucky at the same time. She pretended to be over the moon, but in her heart she cried out for help. She loved Ned and she was determined to stay with him for as long as she could possibly be and make the most of every minute with him. She was deliriously happy with Ned.

After her weekend at home with parents and meeting all her relatives Kay set off for the nurse's home. She was excited to come back. She was looking forward to meet Ned and spend quality time with him. Her sister dropped her at the train station and just before the train departed Kay called Ned to let him know she has left so that he would meet her in central London. In the train all her relatives' speech to her was ringing in her ears. Her emotions were in turmoil. She was happy with Ned and that is all she could think of. She fell asleep on her way back until London. She woke up when everyone was getting off. As usual she was heavily packed although it was for the weekend only. At a distance she saw Ned waving at her. She could not run but she made it as quick as she could and dropped all her luggage and jumped on him. Hugging and kissing, one would think they had been away for a year. Anyhow, Ned took her suitcase and they walked to the underground train station hand in hand. They could not keep themselves apart for a single minute. They were like lovers from the movies. Kay told Ned about her meeting with her parents but did not say anything about family meetings, as she did not want to upset him. All she told him was that her parents were worried that she would be in a strange country and away from them for the first time. They needed reassuring that everything was planned and that she would not be left stranded. Ned reassured her about that and they were very contented and looked forward for their trip then onwards. They got back to the nurses' home and they went straight to bed for wild sex. It only got better every time. They were both tired from the journey and they went to sleep separately.

Time went by and they both studied and worked hard and were busy planning their holiday. Ned had the most planning to do, as he had to make sure that Kay was safe during her visit and also had to educate his parents, brothers and sisters about European ways of life so that there would be understanding on both side.

So Ned called his parents once a week to tell them about the do's and don'ts of the English ways. It was difficult to start with and it took him a long time to do that. He told them about Kay so that they knew her as much as possible before her arrival and also informed them from the spicy hot food to toilet rolls. He was satisfied with his parents as hospitality was without competition in his family. He knew they would receive her well and welcome her into the family. They knew that Kay was his girlfriend and she would be welcomed as girlfriend. Whereas Kay learned about Ned's brothers and sisters, not in too great details as Ned did not want to overload her with unnecessary information. Kay was not bothered about not having a good time as she knew that she would and she never had any problems knowing and getting on people in new environment. Ned called his parents regularly until the eve of their departure. He was stressed as he wanted everything to be perfect for his beloved. The night before their departure Kay's father called the nurses' home to speak to Kay. She was not found in her room. Her dad then called Ned's extension and found Kay there. He did not make any fuss about why she was there. Instead he spoke to her very kindly and wished her a happy holiday and asked her to call home every now and then to inform them about her well-being. After speaking to Kay, he asked for Ned. Kay got Ned over and they spoke for a while. Kay's father and Ned talked about Kay's safety during her days away. Ned reassured him that all precautions were taken so that the holidays would be safe and outstanding and memorable. Also he informed him that they had both taken travel insurance should anything go wrong. Following their dialogue, Kay's mum spoke to Ned and then she spoke to Kay. The conversation was polite and gratifying, as her parents did not want to lose her to a foreigner. After talking to the parents, Kay and Ned went to the club and met everyone. They had a good time and of course almost everyone was jealous about Kay's holiday with Ned. Everyone in the club wished to be as lucky as Kay. Nevertheless they had plenty of drinks and danced. Ned arranged with Shah to drop them at the airport the following day. After the club, Ned and Kay went for a walk to the park. They sat there for a long time and they talked about a lot of things from holiday to finishing their course. Kay was feeling a bit sad as Ned was completing complete his course a year before her and she was worried that they would separate and their experience would have been a college-time romance. Ned reassured Kay that no matter where he would end up working he would never be too far from her. They both held each other very tight and stayed there for an hour at least. Following their chat, they came to Kay's room. Kay had kept a bottle of wine for the evening as she knew that she would get a separate room in Ned's parent's house and that sex would be difficult. She did not mind it as the holiday and the experience for her outweighed more than sex. So they settled in with the television on and started with the bottle of wine. Half way through the wine they were both undressed, in their birth suit and all over each other. Sex was energetically exciting. They attempted all position in one night and tried to make lovemaking as long as possible. They both put so much emotion in it that the pleasure at the orgasm was enormous. It was so good that Kay cried her eyes out, and Ned remained there lying in dreams. It was so good and satisfying that it was out of this world. They stayed there for sometime in each other's arms then Ned left, as they had to have a good rest prior to the departure. Ned struggled to his room and went to bed whereas Kay fell asleep straight away. They were both pleased with their companionship.

18

The big day, the day they were leaving England finally arrived. Kay and Ned were very excited. Kay was about to have her experience of her life and Ned was going to meet his parents and introduce his girlfriend. They were both looking forward to it. Shah picked them up from their room and loaded their luggage in Ned's car. Shah drove them to Heathrow. He dropped them off at the departure drop off point; they said their good byes and Shah left. Kay and Ned went to check in with their luggage and afterwards they went to the departure lounge hand in hand. They were being watched by everyone as they were of different origin, colour, and culture. In the departure lounge, they were sitting together and waiting, hand in hand and shoulder to shoulder. Kay got few stares and repulsive looks from the English workers at the airport and Ned got some stares and stinking looks from fellow travellers from his country. Obviously, they disapproved although there are so many mixed marriages and relationships in England. It was funny to them but Kay and Ned felt quite normal and comfortable. They refused to let go of their hands just because people were staring at them. When the boarding of their flight was announced they went in and settled in the plane.

Luckily they had two seats for themselves and there were nobody next to them. They were comfortable and settled down.

During the beginning of their flight they kept getting weird looks of disapproval. However, after the meal was served in the plane, everyone seemed to settle down for a sleep. The television was showing a film that no one seemed interested in. Kay and Ned had few glasses of wine and were hot for sex. Ned made the tricky suggestion. Neither of them had this experience of sex in public before except for the park. Especially in the plane, that was only heard of but never known whether it was true or not. Kay was not happy about it but the alcohol effect was speaking on her behalf. They both agreed that they would try no matter what the circumstances were. If they were caught they could not be thrown out, as it was a direct flight. They waited for the lights to go off altogether. When all the movement stopped they started. They covered themselves with their blankets and folded the arm-rest that was separating them. Their seat belts were off by then. Ned fondled with Kay's breast until she was well relaxed while she held to his manhood until he was well ahead in the mood. Ned whispered to Kay to remove her knickers while she was still fully clothed. So, she skilfully slipped out of her knickers and pulled her dress up to her waist. Meanwhile Ned pulled his trousers and underwear down to his knees. They had to work out how to proceed. That did not take much as every move was well coordinated. They loved foreplay and would not make love without it. That ensured Kay had a good orgasm every time. So first of all Kay lowered herself onto Ned's lap as if she was having a nap with her head well covered. But little did anyone know what was going on. She was giving Ned a good time while Ned was bent over her waist with his hands doing a good job and keeping Kay interested in hers. They had to be very discreet and also not to make any noise. The airhostesses and stewards kept walking up and down answering calls and checking on the customers. They never noticed anything. After a good 15 minutes, they changed position. This time Ned was having a tasteful nap while Kay held on tight to his organ. She was enjoying great pleasure and was giving fulfilling and quiet squeaks. She could not help not moaning as she always enjoyed sex. After another 15 minutes of moaning and wriggling her body on the chair Ned got up. They stopped for few seconds and thought about the next position to facilitate penetration. Ned raised his head up and still no one paid any attention to what they were doing. So, he calmly changed his position. He lied on the chair as if he was sleeping side by side with Kay. Then Kay got in so that Ned was sleeping behind her. They both covered suitably and they looked like real lovers sleeping tightly. Underneath the blankets some other things were fitting in proficiently and tightly. He had penetrated Kay from behind and they were settled in gentle slow moves. They held each other very tightly and the more excited they got the hold was becoming tighter. They were at it for a good 30 minutes when suddenly Kay whispered that she could not hold it any longer. Ned asked her to let go of her orgasm and that he was near as well. As soon as Kay let go of herself, she started cuming with fulfilling slow moans. That was extremely exciting for Ned and he had his orgasm at the same time. He was moaning and groaning at the same time. They finished and they remained in that position about an hour so that nobody would doubt and then Kay got up and went to the toilet with her knickers folded in her hand. When she came back, Ned went to the toilet and had a wash. Following their kinky experience they settled down sitting hand in hand and watched the television. They were both relaxed and not worried about anything at all. They were in another world.

The flight went very quick for them. They landed safely and they passed through immigration quickly, collected their luggage and they went out. Walking out was a dream for Kay. She was so excited she could not wait to get out on the streets outside the airport. For Ned it was the first time he came back home to see the family and friends. He could not wait to see everyone especially his mum. They dragged their luggage and there they were already feeling the heat. The sun was shining high in the blue sky. For Kay that was luxury coming from the north of England where all she ever enjoyed was cardigan weather. She looked up and gave Ned a big hug of appreciation. Meanwhile Ned's parents were looking at them at a distance. They were desperately waiting for him too. They also could see Ned and Kay were thrilled to bits that they liked each other. They could tell that they were a couple made and meant for each other. Other native people were looking at them, some of them jealous and some of them very angry that he was in company of a white woman. But for them two it was no big deal. Ned looked out for his parents. He could not see anyone from his family so he decided to wait by the side of the main entrance. Little did he know that his family were looking at him for a while but they could not get to him quickly as the airport was unusually busy. However, after few minutes of waiting they were standing next to the parents. There were screams of excitement. Ned was hugging and kissing everyone, one at a time. That was how they behaved in their culture. He gave his mum the biggest and longest hug. She was in tears and could not stop shedding tears of happiness. Meanwhile Kay was watching the closeness of the family and the love and affection they shared. After Ned had his session with his family he introduced Kay. One by one Kay kissed the sisters and sisters in laws and shook the brothers' hands. She got a warm welcome. She also kissed Ned's dad and mum and gave them a hug. To Kay kissing and hugging was part of her growing up with her family and she did not have any problems with that. They all walked to the car park and Kay was surprised when she finally realised about the number of people who came to fetch them. There were six cars altogether and it was like a convoy. Every member of the family came. To Kay it was overwhelming, as she was not used to being with so many people. For Ned it was all exciting, meeting them all and catching up with latest happenings and events in the family and the village. He was talking in his mother tongue and at the same time translating for Kay. His sisters and brothers could all speak English except for his mum and dad. Kay was also holding conversation with the others while Ned was in dialogue with his parents. There were no problems as they were very hospitable people. Kay was enjoying every moment from the start. She started living the experience right from the beginning. To her what she saw in the movies about family coming to the airport to fetch relatives from overseas was as true as she could see it live and also the reception and welcome. She was proud to be there with Ned. They all talked in the car and the rest of them followed.

They reached Ned's home at 4.00 in the afternoon. The day was still hot and the sky was blue. Kay got out of the car first and raised her arms up to the sky to enjoy the sunshine and the heat. Meanwhile the rest of the family got out and unloaded. There were a lot people around so there was no need for Ned and Kay to carry anything over to the house. Ned went in followed by Kay. His mum took Kay with her and with the little words of English she could manage, she introduce her to the room where she would be spending the rest of the time with them. Luckily she was located next to Ned's room. Ned went to his old room and sat in bed reflecting on the time he had spent away and he could feel that nothing had changed. In the mean time his parents and brothers and sisters were busy in the kitchen preparing for dinner. Kay went to the bathroom for a shower. It was rather different from what she was used to in England and hotels. The bathroom consisted of a shower adapted to a tank of gas for hot water. No seat to sit on and no bath to take a dip. However she managed a shower standing. She came out and took herself to the small room next door, the toilet. She looked at it and had to think, "now ... how do I manage that?". It was an Asian toilet. She called Ned for assistance. They closed the door behind and Ned showed her how to sit and deal with it. He got out and waited outside as he knew Kay would have difficulty. After 15 minutes there was no sign of Kay calling, so he asked her if there was any problem. She says, "I am squatting but it is difficult, darling. Anyway, where is the toilet roll? I can't find it". Ned started laughing. He asked her to wait and he went to get one. Unluckily, his parents forgot to buy toilet rolls, as they were not used at home. He rushed to the shop and came back. It was 45 minutes and Kay was waiting in the toilet on her first day. Ned got back and threw the toilet roll from the top and then he left. Kay came out and got in Ned's room. She was killing herself laughing. She could not believe it as for her it was very primitive. She did not realise how lucky she was as there were others who still, in this century, used the toilet outside the house.

Anyhow, Ned refreshed himself and they both went down for dinner together. There was everyone sitting as it was when he left home. His father fed everyone the first spoonful including Kay. Following this they all settled down with their meal. Kay was amazed with the variety and taste of the homemade meal. It was all made from fresh homegrown vegetables. Ned's mum reminded her that, 'the way to a man's heart is through his stomach'. That was no news to Kay as she knew and heard that before but enjoying such meal at home was incredible. In England such meal was only bought in restaurant or of course homemade in an Asian home. She was well impressed. From that time she knew that she would have a good time and would enjoy Ned's family and hospitality. The first day was an impression she would remember, the father's feed, and then the toilet roll.

They finished their meal and then Ned and Kay went for a long walk down the village. Ned showed her few important places that had meanings for him. It was dark and they walked hand in hand. They got back home around 10.00 in the evening. At home, Ned's dad was waiting and they all had tea before retiring to bed. The first day was simple and amiable. Kay and Ned were so tired that they went to bed straight away and fell asleep.

19

The next day, early in the morning, Ned got up and went downstairs. He sat next to his mother who was busy preparing breakfast. His mother insisted that he went to bed for prolonged rest as he did not have that luxury living on his own in England. Ned insisted that he wanted to help and live the life that he missed so much being way from home. He hugged his mum and helped just like old days. This brought back memories and his mum burst in tears. Nevertheless they carried on until breakfast was ready. Meanwhile Kay was up and was in the bathroom struggling to sort herself out. She managed without making a scene. She came downstairs and saw Ned sitting next to his mum on the floor and they were talking. They were so deeply engrossed in their conversation that they did not see Kay approaching. And Kay was enjoying the sight so much she did not want to disrupt. She could not understand a word but she knew that they were sharing important moments together. She was appreciating every moment watching him and was thinking that if every son was like Ned then it would be a beautiful world to live in. After few minutes Ned turned around and was surprised to see Kay sitting peacefully at the table. He asked her to come nearer and join in. Kay came, ignored the chair and sat on the floor next to Ned. His mother held her hand and asked her about her first impression of the family. Ned translated every word. Kay was very pleased and felt privileged to be in such a loving and caring family. She liked staying by Ned indeed. Afterwards the rest of the family came down and they shared their breakfast. It was lovely having everyone sitting for breakfast and every meal together. They chatted to Kay as she was the centre of attention.

The day was just beginning. Ned took Kay to the city for a bus ride. They walked around with lots of awkward looks. They did not care about what other people thought as long as Kay and Ned parents were happy. So they were. They had a marvellous day and came back home tired. After dinner they went to bed early. The next day they planned a day at the seaside. The plan was that the whole family would go. Early in the morning the picnic was prepared hand in hand and they all set off. Kay was surprised as to how many people could get in a car. There were four cars and about 30 people altogether. She was not used to this type of piling in the car. It felt like the car was never full enough as more and more kept getting in. At the seaside the cars were unpacked with people and their food. It was amazing to see how much food was prepared for all the people. To Kay the amount was enough for 100 of them. However, they were all big eaters. She enjoyed the sight and the experience. She kept asking Ned a lot of questions about the driving and number of people in the cars and many more about the people she acquainted with during the day. She was concerned about how they would all be controlled with so many children running at the seaside. Ned reassured her that this was a minor outing for them and that a normal would incorporate about 100 people. He asked Kay to relax and concentrate on having a good time. So she did. She got in her swimming suit and ran in the extraordinary warm blue water. Ned followed her. They had a great time in the water with the others joining in. Some were in their swimming suit, some in bikinis and some in their full clothing. They enjoyed their first swimming session and then had lunch. After a long walk down the beach and picking up corals and shells they went for another swim. Kay was surprised at the time she spent in water but was very pleased to be there with Ned and her family. They finished their day late in the afternoon and got back home. It was a great day out and they were so tired that straight after supper they all went to bed.

The holiday was going very well. They enjoyed the weather and the sea. Kay experienced the ways of life and living with a family. It was, to her knowledge, very primitive, although she never mentioned that to Ned. One evening after their long walk home at night, they thought about having a quiet drink at home. Although they had alcohol in Ned's home, yet they never got drunk like they used to in the nurse's home. So, Ned had an idea. He went to the local shop and bought a small bottle of vodka and lemonade. He mixed the drinks on the road so that there would be no suspicion as they were treated with respect. And they had to maintain that level of respect and dignity. So, they got back, met the parents for the usual cup of tea. They had a chat about general matters and waited for the parents to go to bed. As soon as Ned's mum and dad retired, they started with their 'lemonade'. Ned had some Bombay mix that they both liked. That tasted ultra good with alcohol. They enjoyed the drinks and the little private time together. They were feeling very frisky with their vodka and could not keep their hands off each other. After all they had no personal time with all the touring and visiting.

So Ned had to think quickly as he did not want the parents to know that sex was involved in their relationship as in their culture it was taboo to have sexual encounter outside marriage. He was drunk but knew exactly what he wanted. Therefore, without realising he put the bottle of drinks together with the other drinks in the kitchen cupboard. Kay and him took a walk outside. It was full moon. They could not think where to have sex without risking a show. They looked around and were getting desperate. There were houses all around. Suddenly Ned had an idea. He went at the back of the house, and climbed the tree that was next to the house. Kay followed and they were on top of the house. They were not to be seen from there. So they undressed quickly and got engaged in wild sex. Kay was trying her best not to make any noise but could not help it as she was enjoying repetitive multiple orgasms. It was a special time. Ned was keeping very quiet whilst enjoying the session.

Meanwhile, Ned's brother was awake with the noise Kay was making but little did he know what it was and where it was coming from. All he could hear was the squeaks. Half asleep, he was walking around the house to see what it was. He came out and could hear something on top of the house. So to scare whatever it was he threw some pebbles, whatever he picked from the ground. When Kay got a shower of pebbles on her back she stopped and jumped off Ned who, straightaway, gathered what that meant and pushed his palms on her lips to keep her quiet. They waited quietly and Ned peeped down to see if the person has gone. He looked and saw that it was his brother. So they remained quiet for a while until he ensured that he was gone then they continued with their passionate love-making. They finished and then they went down to the house. They got in their bedrooms quietly and saw each other in the morning.

At breakfast, everyone was talking about the noise on top of the house. Some thought it was the cats, some thought it was the bat and some thought it was something to do with loose spirits. They were all so serious about it that they were going to keep a watch for this unusual occurrence. Kay and Ned kept quiet throughout this conversation, as they knew what the cats, the bats and the loose spirits were up to last night. After breakfast they went out on their trip to visit the museum and in the bus they could not stop laughing. But one thing they were sure about was that they could not have sex there again although it was romantic and great. So everyday, in order to avoid becoming frisky in the evening they has sex either in the bathroom when everyone was out or in the sea. They had a great time. Two days before the end of their holidays there was a dinner party where everyone was invited. There was a lot of friends and family. They all had a big homemade meal and a lot of savoury snacks. They chatted a lot about life there and in England. Funnily people who never had travelled asked Kay why she was not walking topless on the streets here as other tourists did. They also asked Ned whether he saw topless women walking down the streets in England. Kay was surprised by those questions but not Ned, as he knew where they were coming from. The tourists gave different impressions of themselves and gave their country a bad reputation due to the way they dressed on holiday, which represented the way they behaved and dressed in their homeland. Kay was very disappointed that such was the conception of tourists as it was not the case but she understood why it was. She talked a lot about England, the way people behave and dress but it was difficult to convince the natives as they always saw those drunken behaviours, sex on the beach and walking topless away from the beach and partner swapping on holidays too many a time. For Kay it was sad that people had such impressions of the visitors. Nevertheless she maintained that it was not the case and continued socialising. She did not take those comments to heart as she knew that those behaviours were of holiday-makers. After the dinner, very late at night, to Kay's and Ned's surprise, came a group of singers and dancers. Ned's father arranged it so that Kay got an idea of the culture as she already knew about the songs and music. Kay was pleasantly surprised. The dancing and singing started. Everyone joined in and Kay was taken aside by the sisters and was assisted to get dressed in the cultural outfit. She looked beautiful and one in a million. She joined in the dancing and there was Ned sitting there in shock. He could not believe that Kay would look so stunning. He was there enjoying the scene. After a while the men joined in and Ned and Kay danced together for a long time. Kay was well settled in the hip gyrating movement and was combining the cultural dance with the hip hop and house music. It was excellent. It was late indeed. Then Ned noticed that his mum and dad were dancing as well. He was surprised, just like all others. He stood there and watched. Nobody could understand, but then there was the bottle of lemonade next to the spot where they were sitting! It all made sense to Ned. The bottle was empty and that was a blessing in disguise, as the parents could not get drunk anymore than they were. So skilfully he went and picked the bottle and discarded it so that it would not bring up questions. The evidence eliminated, Kay and Ned got in the dance and danced the night away. The party was great and ended around 5.00 in the morning. They were all sleeping everywhere, on the floor, the sofa, hanging on the chairs. They remained wherever they collapsed. That was the best party ever in their house and best of all was the parents participating in the dancing, something that never happened in the past.

The day before leaving for England, Kay and Ned went to the restaurant in town with the whole family. They enjoyed a meal and came back home very late. At home there was a speech by his parents and all brothers and sisters. What they talked about was very emotional. They talked about Ned and his effort towards making his life a success and they also talked about Kay. They told Kay that they were proud of her and were happy to have her. She was a talented girl with lots of potential and they could see her making Ned very happy should she wish to join the family. There was absolutely no pressure on any aspect of their relationship. They accepted Kay the way she was and they enjoyed having her around. Kay thanked them for their hospitality and showed her appreciation for everything they did. Kay was so emotional during her speech that she burst in tears. She was very sad indeed but as she put it "that's life, good things never last long". After all the speech was completed, Ned's mum offered Kay to have henna put on her palms. Kay never liked anything written on her hands let alone putting henna which would last longer than two weeks. As she was so satisfied with her holidays she accepted this offer. Ned was pleasantly surprised to Kay's acceptance. He called her privately and confirmed her decision. She seemed to be ready for it. So Ned's mum painstakingly put henna in Kay's both palms and after that she went to bed. Ned stayed up and talked to his mum and dad for a long time. They were all pleased with Kay and him although they told him that he should be weary of people who did not like mixed relationship. Ned reassured his parents that Kay was good for him but the decision to get married to her was not in his mind at that time. He did not want to promise anything to his parents, as he knew the score from Kay's parents' behaviour. He went to bed very late.

The day of their departure, Kay got up early and got herself washed and dressed. Ned followed. They were the first to get up that morning. They had breakfast and they took tea for everyone in their bed. Ned's mum was emotional with that gesture that she burst in tears. She looked at Kay and took her hands and looked at the henna's effect, "your husband will love you very much", she said. Kay just smiled. Ned explained that the darker the drawing with the henna meant the more she would be loved by the man she would marry. Once the family had their breakfast, Kay and Ned got ready and packed. It was early but they had to be ready as they expected a lot of people to visit before they left for the airport. From 1.00 in the afternoon until 5.00 in the afternoon they had lots of visits and they received a present from every visitor. They did not refuse anyone their presents but they could not carry more than what they had packed already. So, they had to leave the presents behind. Ned's parents were aware of the difficulties of travelling with excess weight and the fines attached to it. So they discreetly kept the presents back and gave them to others who would use them.

They all left for the airport. Saying good-bye to Kay and Ned was difficult. Not only that they had to hire an eighty seater bus to accommodate anyone who wanted to accompany them but they also had to kiss and hug, and say few words before going. The whole experience of going back got harder and there were a lot of tears to go with it. Kay was surprised with all the love and attention she received.

The good-bye session was made very quick as they had to check in. Ned and Kay ran for the waiting room as the last announcements were made. The family members returned home and Ned and Kay headed for England. They were pleasantly tired with their time away together with the family. Kay was in tears and was missing all the fuss around her. They just sat in the plane during their return. No sex or excitement. They were very quiet and slept after their meal.

20

The plane landed and they went through immigration very fast and then picked up their luggage. They walked out hand in hand. At the arrival they were expecting Shah but to their surprise they saw Kay's parents as well. That was a shock. As soon as they saw her parents they let go of their hands but little did they know that they were already seen. They came out and were welcome by Shah who was standing next to Kay's parents. Kay jumped on her dad's neck and expressed how much she missed them. Ned was standing there and did not know what to make of it, because during the holiday she never had any chat about 'missing parents'. Nevertheless he carried on. Kay, and her parents thanked Ned for the time away and they drove to the nurses' home separately. Ned was a bit disappointed with the reception and Kay's behaviour but he accepted it as 'that's how it was'. Shah and Ned drove slowly in the little car huffing and puffing away. They shared valuable information about home and the goings on in England. Shah told Ned about the unexpected visit from Kay's parents in the nurse's home and he was really sorry that he could not inform him. It was too late and again there weren't any phones on the plane but most of all Ned did not expect Shah to inform him. So they just had to wait for the reaction.

In the other car, Kay was telling her parents about her holidays. She told them about the toilet and was cracking jokes about the ways of living and the food and the swimming session with the family. All she was saying in the car was very negative. It was better that Ned did not hear it. Kay always appreciated the time at Ned's parents but making jokes about his family would certainly put Ned off her, as he really loved his parents. They were laughing in the car all the way making fun of the people. Her dad asked her about the colouring in her hands. She told them that she hated it and that she was forced to have the henna on. So she agreed in order to avoid aggravation and that they would not be offended. Ned would not have liked that as he confirmed with her prior to having the henna put on. Kay was so negative it was unbelievable and then summarising the time to her parents, she says, "for a free holiday of a life time, it was the best but I could not take it all over again". Little did Kay know that her parents saw her holding on to Ned's hands at the airport but they chose to say nothing about it. They were ecstatic with the 'taking the mick' session. However, her father asked her about the henna again, "I thought that they only had henna when they were getting married!". Kay's reply was the same as previously and she also told them about the thought behind it. She had a good laugh with them at Ned's expense.

In the little banger, Ned was excited relating his side of the story to Shah. He was so delighted that his parents accepted Kay and told him all about the toilet and the party and the seaside and the speeches. Ned also told Shah how much Kay liked it. Of course, with all the preparation and the rest how could she not like it? He did a lot of work on his family and friends before and during their holiday. He was relaxed knowing that it was successful. Shah was pleased that it all went well and said that he was going to speak to Kay and ask her about her experiences when he met her next time. They arrived to the nurse's home and settled in. Kay was busy with her parents and Ned was busy getting unpacked. At night Kay was still not to be seen. He did not make an issue about it as he thought of giving her the space as they have spent a long time together. So in the evening he went to see Shah, they had dinner and then headed for the social club. When they got in they saw Kay and her parents in there having a drink and a chat. They were surrounded with few friends and external members of the social cub. As soon as they saw Ned and Shah, they stopped and dispersed. Kay's parents continued socialising. Kay came to say hello to Ned and Shah and invited them to join her parents. So, after getting their drinks they joined them. They started talking about the holidays. Ned was quiet and was listening to Kay's experience. She said she had great time. Ned was happy about it and the dialogue was very short. There was a silence, so Shah and Ned walked to the bar and sat there for their drinks as usual. They finished and went to their rooms. Kay's parents stayed until the next day.

The days went by until one evening Shah came to Ned in a rush and asked him for more detailed account of his holidays. Ned was taken aback with that request.

Shah was not going to say it, but reluctantly he did tell Ned about Kay's comments about her holiday and that they were being ridiculed in the club. Shah knew well about how much Ned was in love with Kay so he tried not to make an issue of it. Shah decided that nothing should be done about it as there was no point and that Ned should be aware of what to expect when he went to the club. After talking to Shah, Ned went to see Kay and asked her general questions about the subject. Kay denied everything and emphasised how much she enjoyed the holidays. Ned made no comments and went to Shah, they then went to the club. As soon as they walked in they were welcome with laughter with the toilet story. That was enough to confirm Ned's thoughts about Kay. He was very disappointed but they made a joke about it and carried on as usual. Ned did not say anything to Shah either as he did not want anything to come between their friendship, especially a woman. They were like brothers and that's how it should remain. He went back to his room. He could not study as this issue was troubling him. He started to have great doubts about Kay and several questions crossed his mind. Was it all about a free holiday? Was it about good sex? Was it about being with someone that everyone is proud of at college? Or lastly was it about being with someone with good reputation? He did not know what to think anymore. He was saddened indeed and went to sleep without seeing Kay. He was in love with Kay and he had to deal with it. But how? He did not know. Kay also did not come to visit him that night. So Ned decided not to tell Kay much more and stopped helping her with her studies and reducing the amount of time that he spent with her. He decided that he would wait Kay's next move to know what is going on in her mind.

Once Ned started acting on his decision, he did not see any difference in Kay's behaviour. She still gave him the same attention and love as before. Therefore, there was no effect on her relationship with him. So he decided to forgive her and carry on as normal, after all it was his life. What was important to him was what he had seen on holidays. However, that was another lesson learnt; he would never take anyone on holiday home with him again, no matter how sincere the friendship.

Life in the nurse's home went as usual, party, drinks, and explorative sex were always on menu. Kay and Ned worked hard through the semester until their next holiday. They grew so close that a weekend away was too much to cope with. Kay's parents asked her to join them on their family holiday to but she was too involved with Ned, hence, she refused. Instead she wanted to go to Minehead with Ned. So they booked a caravan when her parents went to Turkey. They stayed in the holiday park and spent a great time for the first week. They had the entire caravan for themselves and had sex everywhere possible. They went to restaurant everyday for their meals and enjoyed a bottle of wine before bed. It was luxury for them. During the day they explored Somerset and Devon. They went to the Cheddar Caves and drove around Lynmouth and the nearby interesting places. They walked down Brean beach every afternoon. They went to Land's End and walked everywhere on the cliffs and took lots of memorable pictures. It was the time of their life. It could not have been better with romantic evenings and meals. No social club and friends. It was out of the ordinary, cheap, simple but effective. They left Minehead after their first week and drove to Kay's home in the north as her parents were away for two weeks. The old banger survived the drive.

They reached Kay's home in the afternoon and settled in for a rest. Her neighbours saw Ned's car in the drive and were peeping to see what was happening. Their sights were glued to the driveway until the next morning to monitor Ned's and Kay's activities. The next morning as soon as Ned and Kay got out of the house to go to the shops, the neighbours from both sides got in their drive and started talking to Kay. They asked her how she was and how it happened that she was there. Nothing about Ned was asked but the message was clear that they saw Ned staying over. Kay was not a fool and she knew precisely what they were up to, checking on her. So, she told them that Ned was staying for couple of days with her as they had some works to do. From that time onwards Kay knew what to expect when her parents came. Regardless, she carried on in the company of Ned. They went out and about for the week and visited places. She introduced Ned to the Midlands and the beautiful areas with history. Ned was very impressed with Kay and the way things were going on. In the evening, they spent the night on the double bed, a luxury they only enjoyed in the caravan until then. It was great. They had sex openly in the house as there was nobody around. On the eve of her parents return she tidied the whole house including Ned's body hairs and washed everything they used. She eliminated all factors that would make her parents suspicious of any activities although they would know about it from the neighbours. Then Ned left for the nurse's home.

Kay was nervous about the return of her parents and the feedback from the neighbours. Courageously, she went to the airport to pick them up. On the way back they had their usual 'catching-up' dialogue. Then Kay told them about Ned's stay with her. She was honest about everything except the relationship. The parents exchanged some looks but as usual they said nothing - that was the plan. They agreed to everything and mentioned that it was okay although they would rather have him around when they were there. Nothing much said about the subject and they returned home as normal. As soon as they settled down, the neighbours rang one by one. They spoke for a long time on the telephone. The parents knew for definite that Kay was seeing Ned in a very intimate way. They decided not to make an issue of it hoping that their indirect pressure would put a stop to the relationship.

After the weekend Kay was returning back to the nurse's home. So they planned a family get together. Kay knew about it and was fine. At least it was not unexpected and there was nothing like the previous meeting. The whole family turned up for the meal and they had a good old chat about the old days. It was all meant to remind Kay about the family's values. Little did she know what it was all about. So, she enjoyed her meal and meeting everyone. There were lots of general questions about her holidays and life with Ned's parents. She told them about her lifetime experience and had a good laugh. She made them feel as if Ned was not important to him and she was very convincing too. Afterwards, she got ready early to leave as she was desperate to go and see Ned. She missed him badly and wanted to have him around her. The rest of the guests were sitting in the lounge talking about their holidays and forthcoming events. Before leaving she made a cup of tea in the kitchen for herself and joined the others. They were talking about her sister's marriage as she had been engaged for a long time. They were planning the wedding in general and then, her mother said "Kay, it would be lovely to see you on the aisle on your big day". Kay was a little bit shocked and did not know what to say. So she kept quiet and smiled as if the comment was of no importance. Her mother asked, "when are you going to settle down? We would like to meet the man of your life. Very soon you will finish your nursing and will be working your life away". She said nothing and continued drinking her tea. Then her grandmother said, "I would like to see your beautiful church wedding at least before I die love". "It will be. Do not worry. I am not worried about it at the moment. Time will tell what it will be. At the moment I am more interested in completing my course successfully", Kay replied. She smiled to everyone while talking and continued, "I do not want to be on the shelves you know. I am working on it. Let me live life a bit first". Everyone laughed although there was nothing to laugh about the comment. She finished her drink and then said goodbye and left with her dad. There was not much of a conversation in the car. The parents knew what they were up to and were putting indirect pressure on Kay for a re-think. To them they were not doing anything wrong by expecting her to marry and live with a Caucasian man. However, they did not realise what Kay's emotions were like. Or may be nobody knew what Kay felt like as she never said it. What she told Ned was true or untrue, only she would know. After all she knew exactly what she wanted from her life. Whatever was in her mind did not matter as she was in love with Ned. But, she did not fight her family to be with Ned. On the other hand Ned was very much in love and charmed by her, so jubilant that he did not want anything else from life for as long as he had Kay next to him. They were both very lively and the relationship was progressing positively.

Kay got back to the nurse's home late that evening due to some engineering works on the rail tracks. Ned was waiting for her at the station. They got back and went their separate ways as they were both tired. They promised to see each other the next day for some quality time. The next day they saw each other and the rest of the semester continued. Ned was finishing his course as he came to the end of his third year and Kay had to stay for the last year. After graduating Ned got a very good job in the community in a prestigious private company. He continued to see Kay daily although he lived in central London. They lived life as normal couple would live and did everything together. There were never any fights or arguments. It was a relationship made in heaven. They always thought they were soul mates and it did look so from outside. They went to holidays together and when Kay's parents were away they were in Kay's house having a great time. They went on caravan holidays every time they had the opportunity.

21

In his new job, Ned was treated well due to his original ideas and he developed the service very quick. He was promoted fast within the company and enjoyed his first company car after six months. Kay was impressed and obviously her parents knew about Ned performance. Talking about Ned was a normal thing. There was no pressure about it or negativity around it. Her parents were genuinely impressed by him but that did not change their mind although they always encouraged Kay to follow in his footsteps. He was good enough for anything except to join the family. That was very clear. In her third year Kay went on holidays with Ned openly 'as a very good mate'. Her parents knew about it and they did not dare oppose just in case they would not be worthy of Kay's love. But then things changed.

The academic year ended and Kay graduated. Her parents came to her graduation and so did Ned. All was good as the last year at college was great for Kay. There were no problems encountered and so was the last day. They all had a superb time and went for a drink to say good-byes to their friends and there were addresses and telephone numbers exchanged. There were tears and speeches. Some were sobbing and some were laughing their heads off. The party and the buffet were brilliant. By the afternoon it was all over. Ned was not sure what to do afterwards as the parents were still there and he planned so stay with Kay that night. Nothing was spoken. So he played the game. Kay's mum asked, 'what time are you going to London? Hope you will not miss the train!''. Ned had to think carefully about the answer as he did not want to ruin anything on the last day. "I am going to the nurse's home first and meet Shah before I get back. In any case I am off tomorrow", he replied. Kay was quiet and said nothing. So Kay's father called a mini-cab and they went to the nurse's home, and Ned followed in another mini-cab. They reached their destination around the same time. Ned said good-bye to Kay and he was off to see Shah.

Kay went to her room and her parents and herself were getting ready to go to the restaurant to celebrate. Ned was not invited as it was a family celebration. He did not know about that. Innocently he came and knocked at Kay's door. Her father answered the door. "Oh Ned! Kay is getting ready. Do you want to wait" said Kay's dad. "I do not mind. I will wait", replied Ned. So the door was shut on his face as he waited. It was a very long wait as he was waiting for his loved one. So after few minutes he knocked again. Her mum answered the door. "Sorry Ned. But you know how women are with getting ready to go out", said her mum. "Anywhere interesting?", asked Ned. "We are going to an Indian restaurant, you know, family meal together to celebrate the occasion", replied Kay's mum. "That's great. In that case I will not wait. I do not want to hold you. My apologies. Please inform Kay that I will be in touch on my next visit to the nurse's home", said Ned. They finished their short conversation and Ned left, very disappointed. He was not disappointed because he was not invited, or he did not know of the plan afterward but because Kay did not even bother to come out to say hello. After all they were in one room only, standard nurse's home's room. He could not understand why she did not come. It was so simple.

Meanwhile Kay could hear all the conversation but was not interested and signalled her parents to push him away. She commented that Ned was the best person to have as friend in the nurses home. But she did not think inviting him for dinner was the best thing to do on the last day. She told her mum that she had not told him that she was leaving the nurse's home for good in the next week. Of course for her parents it was good news and they were happy with that. After all they were confident with their daughter.

However, Ned took a slow walk to Shah and related the story to him. Shah said he was not surprised as he overheard many of Kay's conversation with her friends. But he did not explain. Ned got worried and asked Shah whether there was another man. Shah reassured him that there was no one else as far as he knew. If there was anyone else he would have notified him straight away. Ned was satisfied with the information and did not ask any other questions. They had supper in the canteen and went to the club. Shah and Ned had a lot to drink and were both heavily drunk. Although Ned was drunk, he was still in control and thinking straight. He asked Shah what he meant about Kay earlier. Ned stressed that he had been seeing her almost every time he had time off from work and that he had not seen or noticed anything different. Shah never lost his marbles while drinking either and felt sorry about Ned's situation. So he gave a good speech, "Ned, you are the best friend I have ever had in England. I might tell you something that you won't like and Kay might deny. I do not want to lose you as my friend. I know you will say that you will not refuse me your friendship, but believe me when one is in love, one is blind. But you are the best I have known…(there is silence)… Ned, I could say you were taken for a good ride, but I can also say that Kay loves you dearly… (silence)… if you want to know what it is what, come this week before Saturday and ask Kay how she feels about you". Shah caught Ned by his neck and asked to retire. They went to Shah's room and Shah slept on the floor and Ned was offered the bed. That was hospitality. They slept.

Meanwhile Kay and her parents were enjoying an Indian meal at Ned's favourite restaurant. They had a good meal and Kay spoke to them openly about her plans for the future. She also talked about Ned and all his help towards finishing her course. She said she would keep in touch with him as he was a great guy and intelligent and a good mover. Her mother looked at her and asked, "what do you mean?". "Ned was the most famous and wanted person in the nurse's home and he was the most adored man in college. He was a great dancer and was never short of offers from women when he went out. We used to call him and still call him, the sexy mover. To have him as a close friend was luxury, something that I had and everyone else starved from", she replied. They laughed about it and continued with their meal. They got back around midnight and they all stayed in Kay's room.

In the morning Ned got up early and went straight to work. In the nurse's home Kay's parents stayed until lunch and then left. Her parents were happy and Kay was over the moon indeed having achieved her aim to be a nurse. She went to the club every evening and met with her friends and they continued celebrating. They went to the night club and went for dinners. During that time she did not bother calling Ned as she was busy having a good time. She met Shah almost every day and nothing was spoken about her love life and she did not even say what she was going to do career wise. Shah was not surprised, as he knew what was going on through other people but left it for Ned to find out for himself.

The week went by very quick and Ned had been busy with work. He called Kay but she was never in for a chat. He missed her very much. So he decided that he would visit on Friday evening after work and planned to stay and have the week end off. So he did.

He turned up on Friday evening. He took himself to Kay's room and knocked at the door. There was no reply. He left a note on her notepad. He looked from outside and her curtain was drawn and it was very quiet. So he went to visit Shah. He was not in the room. So he went to the club. Neither Kay nor Shah were there. So he stayed there in the hope that they would come back before he decided to leave. After two hours of sitting in the club, Shah came. He had been out for a meal with colleagues at work. He was pleased to see Ned. They hugged and they sat down for the usual chat. It was already 11 o'clock at night. They had few drinks and then they left. Ned told Shah that he was looking for Kay but she was nowhere to be found. Shah was not surprised and told Ned about the girls' night out all week. There were no men involved but they were having a good time after the stressful three years. "That's great. I understand. The funny thing is that she is never in when I call", said Ned. "Well, check later if she is in. If she is not then stay with me, you know the door is always open for you", suggested Shah. "Thanks", said Ned. The club was closing and they left. Shah reminded Ned that he would be there should he need a space to put his head down. Ned appreciated Shah's offer but he was determined to visit Kay. He was not going back unless he had seen her. He missed her for long enough and after the experience on the graduation day, they needed to speak. So Ned went to Kay's room again. She was not in. So he went for a walk to the town. He was drunk and merry but was also worried about the future with Kay. On the way, he met Kay and her mates returning from their night out. All the girls were drunk. They saw Ned and they cheered. Kay came onto Ned and jumped on him and said how much she missed him. Ned was desperate for that hug and kiss. They hugged for a long time and kissed. Her friends continued walking. Ned and Kay walked slowly to the nurse's home. There was nothing that could be discussed or talk about as Kay was clearly drunk. Ned took her to her room and helped her undress and assisted her to bed. They both fell asleep and stayed in bed until late the next day, Saturday.

Kay and Ned both recovered from the previous night. They went to the canteen for lunch. While having lunch other friends of Kay came to say good-bye and wished her all the best. To that Ned was surprised. He could not believe his ears. He remained quiet, as he did not want to have an argument or private discussion in public. So he played the game and pretended that he knew everything. Inside he was getting very angry. Kay was leaving on the day and he was not aware of it. How shocking!

After lunch they went to her room. They walked together hand in hand. Kay did not say anything about going back home. She was behaving as if there was nothing different, just normal. They got in the room. Kay offered Ned a drink as usual and they sat down and talked. Kay still did not say anything although her suitcase was all packed and she hardly had anything in the room. Ned could not bear it any longer, so he asked "do I take it you are going back home". "Yes darling", replied Kay. That was all from her. She did not elaborate. Ned was in despair. How could this be that he was not told and why was Kay not keen talking about departing home. His face dropped, with his eyes showing all signs of bursting in tears. But he was not going to. He was angry more than anything else. He contained himself and asked, "so, will I see you again?". Kay was busy packing and replied, "if you want to see me then yes, you know I am fond of you". She did not even look back and continued with her task. Ned was getting confused by the minute. Before, she was so much in love and could not be without him and then in her reply she was very fond of him and if he wanted to visit then she would have him. Ned was in love, not lust and he was going down with this love story of his life. What was happening? He could not work it out. Love is blind. So he thought that no matter what he was not going to lose his love. So he tried again, "Kay do you love me still like you did two weeks ago?". To that Kay came over and sat on Ned's lap. "Of course, I am fond of you and I will always miss you", she replied and then she kissed Ned. Then she went back to her packing. "Okay", said Ned, in that case I do not mind travelling to see you whenever we have time". "Are you sure darling, it is a very long drive as you know!", said Kay. "I do not mind as long as I get to see you", said Ned. "Well, I do not mind, as long as you know that you cannot come every week end and of course my parents are different than I as you know", said Kay.

For Ned everything was getting complicated. In just one week his entire life was turning upside down. Kay clearly did not seem interested and bothered but at the same time she was not being straight with Ned. Although she was going back, she did not say anything about her future plans and how they would manage to see each other. She was just agreeing to what Ned was suggesting. So Ned asked again, "what are you going to do there, job-wise?". "I have got a job as a carer until I get my registration number", she replied. That was interesting, she already had a job to go to whilst she was in the nurses home. So it clicked. "That is interesting and I am very impressed, no wonder you have been very evasive talking about this subject. You know Kay; I think you are doing the right thing. May be it will help in some way in the future. Whatever happens, happens for the best", said Ned. Kay was not expecting such a comment from Ned so she had to calm him down. "I want to be next to my parents and that does not mean that I do not want you. Of course you can visit me and we will keep in touch as much as possible if you want to. There is no need to be sarcastic. We can go away just the same and have a good time just the same. The only difference is that I am not near", said Kay. Hearing her talk in her tender and loving voice, Ned settled down and gained confidence in her reply. They held each other and kissed. Ned was miserable but at least he knew that she was still going to continue with her relationship with him. He said, "well ... in that case I do not mind travelling to come and see you, I miss you very much already and know that I will miss you a lot. I just wished I knew from before". He held Kay tightly close to him and stayed there with his head on her shoulders. Kay returned the intimacy and closeness by stroking his head and kissing him at every opportunity. Suddenly there was a knock at the door.

Kay got up and opened the door. "How nice, you are on time uncle George", screamed Kay with joy. Ned was there sitting looking at her happiness and joy. She was so overjoyed to go home. She introduced Ned to her uncle and as everything was unexpected, he was there to pick Kay up. Ned was disappointed and had to make himself scarce, as it was time for Kay to leave. He felt lonely for a minute and very sad that he did not have enough time to say good-bye and say his last words. This made him feel very bitter about the whole things. So he got up and said, "Okay, so it time to say good-bye. All the best and I wish you a lot of success in whatever you do. Keep happy and smiling and if ever you think about the student-life then keep in touch". He shook Kay's hand and then her uncle's then he walked out. Kay got everything out of her room and got in the car. It was very quick. As soon as Ned left the room she was out and they drove off within ten minutes. She was thrilled to bits and Ned the opposite. There was Ned sitting in his car in the car park, looking at her leaving. He watched until they disappeared. He went in a deep dream thinking about the last happy years and was wondering what would be in the future with Kay. He sat in his car for an hour before he drove off to London. Driving back seemed very long indeed with lot of things in his mind. He got home and first thing first he took his photo album out and revived all the fun time they had together. He looked at them for a long time, digesting every picture, one by one. He took the best one, a picture on the cliffs when they went to Lands End and stuck it on the wall next to his bed. He looked at it every time he rolled over.

Ned was finding it difficult to adjust with the new situation and thought of calling Kay for a chat. Then, after reflecting on the circumstances of Kay's departure, he had a re-think. Although he missed Kay dearly he was going to wait however long it would take for her to call him. One day went by, there was nothing. Second day went by, still nothing. He was getting desperate but was determined to wait. The fourth day there was still no sign of her call.

Meanwhile, ever since Kay went home to her parents, she had been busy settling in her room with all her stuffs that she gathered over the past three years. She was meeting her old friends and renewing her contacts with them. She was out every night. She was working in a residential home as a carer and earning little cash as she was not registered as nurse. At £2.50 per hour she was being used to provide high level of care and also be in-charge of the home. It was a disgrace that she could accept such responsibilities for so low pay. However, she felt comfortable being in the midst of her family. She worked hard and did funny shifts. She knew she was being used and the owner was getting a good deal from her, nevertheless she continued. Kay was having a great time re-adjusting with her old environment and going shopping with her mum. Ned was not talked about at home as everyone thought he was history. They were all so proud that Kay was back.

22

After two weeks of being busy then normality resumed. Novelty wore off and life became normal and routine. Then Kay started missing her life full of excitement in the nurse's home. She looked back in time and then suddenly she thought of Ned, "my god, it had been two weeks!", she exclaimed, "I wonder how he is and getting on?". At last he came to her mind.

In the mean time Ned had been depressed for two weeks. He went to see Shah every night after work. They got drunk every time and he stayed by Shah most of the time, sleeping on the floor and at times in bed. He tried to chat up other girls and went to their bedroom for one-night stand but could not settle with the idea. One-night stand never excited him, so he apologised to every girl he visited and went back home to Kay's picture. It was distressing to look at Ned. Looking at Ned one could not tell that he was not 'right' unless one knew him very well. His behaviour was normal at work. Everyone was envious of him at the work place as they saw him as very stable, with good job, good luck, with good prospects for the future, and of course the good looks. He was never affected in that sense except that his love was not requited. Lucky or unlucky it was debatable, but he was not settled in his personal life. One point he made sure of was that no one at work would ever know of his personal life. So he always was friendly and close to the junior members of staff but never close and friendly enough to tell them about his life. That distance he always kept to protect his work and his reputation. Of course as usual in the workplace there was always rumours that he was sleeping with this one or that one. As it was not true it never bothered him although at time it was quite annoying. His mind and conscience was clear and that was what mattered.

So while Ned has been putting up with all sorts of temptations for two weeks the phone rang at night. Ned's phone number was not available to everyone he knew. He was selective in giving out his details. So normally when the phone would ring he would have a guess as to who it could be. 10 out of 10 he would be right. It was 11.00 o'clock at night. He let the phone ring few times and then tried to think who it could be. It did not strike him at first that it could be Kay as she did not call for the last two weeks. The phone stopped ringing. So dialled 1471 and it was Kay's telephone number. He got goose bumps all over his body. He did not know whether to get excited or not. He put the phone down and waited. It rang again after fifteen minutes. This time he knew it was Kay. He picked the phone up straight away, and said, "hello, Kay". "My goodness, how did you know it was me?", said Kay all excited. "I just knew. As you know, if you really love someone, you just feel it. How are you anyway?", asked Ned. In a big sigh of relief Kay replied, "I am fine. Busy with the job as you know. It is hard work".

"Good to know that you are busy and keeping well" said Ned. "And how are you?", asked Kay. "I am great. Could not be better. Life goes on as usual or as unusual" replied Ned. "So keep well. See you sometimes then", said Kay. "As you wish. Let me know when and I will try to be there", said Ned. They said good night and that was it. They spoke after such a long time and the conversation was so dry. Ned missed Kay very much and he was determined to control himself. On the other side Kay missed Ned but more than that she missed the good time she had with him.

It was a very awkward situation. Kay wanted Ned for the good time and the good sex and Ned wanted Kay for love. Ned made his intention very clear but Kay never put her's in words so she was in a strong position to change her status as she liked. Ned was like a toy in Kay's hands. But as it was love was blind. So after speaking to Kay, Ned called Shah to tell him what happened and wanted to know what he meant about Kay when he met him last time. Shah told Ned about his views of Kay openly and Ned understood Kay's behaviour. Shah told him that she was a user and she used him because he was a good stock and most of all a good dancer and the best in bed. Ned thanked Shah for not telling him that before, as it was the best thing to find out for himself. So he did find out but what next. Kay was far away and Ned wanted to be with her although he knew what the scores were. But he wanted Kay to tell him that with her mouth. After talking to Shah he thought for a while and said aloud to himself, "I will find out for the better even if it takes me few years", and rolled in bed. Next to him was Kay's picture. He looked at it and then took it off the wall and put it in his drawer. He did not love her any less but the picture would go there when he made sure of it.

Few minutes after Kay called again. "What's up?", said Ned. "I do not feel the same without you, Ned!" replied Kay. When Ned heard her saying those words he felt so much better and he started talking more like before. "It is the same here. Life without you is becoming unbearable", said Ned. "I miss you so much. I did not think I would miss you so much when I would be here", said Kay. "Why don't you come to spend a week end here as soon as you can?" suggested Ned. "Well darling you know how it is to work and all. I can't come just yet as much as I would like to. I have to come all the way to London by train and then back then go to work. I will be shattered", replied Kay. What Kay was forgetting was that Ned, despite his full time employment, still made time for her. He knew what was happening but went along with it. Somehow Kay forgot that Ned was in the same situation. So assertively Ned said, "well if you want me you have to make an effort. You forget that I am in the same situation. I don't mind coming half way… compromise would be acceptable". Ned was not going to be used anymore and certainly not abused. They negotiated a day, date and time to meet. But then Kay had an idea, "why don't you come and pick me up and we could go to Wales for the weekend. It is on the way…what do you think?". "I don't mind, but then you have to meet the cost of petrol", said Ned. Kay was surprised to this assertion as Ned was never like that before. He always offered and paid for most things. She could not go back and say no. "You are worth every of my pennies love. Do not worry I will pay for the petrol but half and half if ok with you", said Kay. "That's fine by me" said Ned. The meeting was set. Ned was euphoric that he was going to meet Kay. He very well knew what was going on but he was going on with it and hoped that someday things would work out. And in the process he would make sure that he was not abused. In that particular circumstance he was ready to be used to a certain extent. On the other side Kay was thrilled that she could go back to have a good time with Ned and enjoy sex mostly and the delicious meal out.

After talking to Kay he slept. His days at work went happily. Then came the day to go away. Ned got up early in the morning, got dressed, packed and set off. He left home in London at 6.30 in the morning and drove on the motorway. He stopped at the services to get a paper and some snacks. He continued his journey happily. He got to Kay's driveway. He looked at it and smiled. It reminded him of the comment made before and yet he was there again and again. He got out and knocked at the door. Kay's dad opened the door. He was let in without any sarcastic lines. He was offered tea and cakes. He was made welcome. Ned was rather surprised. Kay's parents were least worried, as they knew their daughter well enough. Kay came down and kissed Ned on the cheeks and said loudly, "oh, my chum is here!". "Chum!", Ned thought, "what the hell is this now with all the excitement". But he did not say anything. He missed Kay very much and he gave her a big hug which was meaningful to him. Kay did not hold back and her hug was just as meaningful. She did not mind although her parents were there. Ned thought that there was a definite improvement there and relaxed his views about Kay. He was satisfied. Her dad brought Kay's suitcase and her carrier bags down and loaded it in the Ned's car. That was unusual and Ned was getting impressed by the minute. Her dad gave Ned a gallon of oil to keep in the car. He checked the car for him to make sure it was all okay. They said good-bye and set off with Kay's parents waving from the street. To Ned everything was getting out of his mind, and confusing him. He decided not to ask Kay anything about the behaviour as he was determined to spend a good weekend. They drove off to Snowdonia. They talked in the car as if nothing happened. They were behaving like they have not been apart. All seemed normal. They joked and laughed as they did in the nurse's home. They missed each other very much, that was very clear. In his mind Ned was trying to work out what was happening. It did not make sense, so he decided to be as before and be with the woman he loved. They drove around and searched for a B&B. Ned stayed in the car while Kay went to get the booking. The landlady did not know that she was receiving a foreign man with Kay. When they got in with their luggage, the lady gave Ned a dirty look. It was clear that he was not liked. Too bad they had paid and they were staying. Ned asked the lady if they could have breakfast a bit late in the morning and they wanted an extended rest due to the long drive. The old lady would not budge. Instead she asserted "if you cannot get up on time for breakfast you just have to miss it or if you would like to, then there is a five star hotel down the road". "Thank you", said Ned. And they went upstairs to their room. Kay could not believe it but then Ned said, "at least she is openly racist which makes it easier for me to deal with.

It is better that way". This comment of Ned affected Kay as she thought of her parents and immediately answered back, " don't be like that, they are my parents". "I am so sorry I did not mean it for your parents. You know me I cannot be sarcastic even if I tried", said Ned. And that was it, they settled down and relaxed. Kay was desperate for sex and could not wait any longer. Straight after shower she was there and in her element. Ned made the most of it too. They made lots of noise in the squeaky bed. The lady downstairs kept looking at the ceiling in the hope that it did not come down with them. The immediate urge was tackled and they went out for a long walk. They stopped at a restaurant and had dinner. They walked everywhere and enjoyed it. They were walking hand in hand like the old days. They came back late and again had more action. It was a beautiful evening for them, having dinner and then passion. The old lady was awake and getting annoyed but there was nothing she could do. Every now and then she would quietly crawl up the stairs and would check if there were items missing in the corridors or the bathroom. She did not trust foreign people whoever it was. Kay and Ned stayed there for the weekend and climbed the mountain. They enjoyed every moment together. During their stay they planned their next meeting. They planned to meet once a month and decided where they would go. It was from Lake District to Wales to Bournemouth to Poole to Devon and Cornwall. Ned was happy and so was Kay as they had a schedule and most of all their relationship was surviving although they were far away. All planned, they left Wales with good memories and clear mind. They both felt light. Ned dropped Kay at home in the evening. Her mum saved them some food which they ate and then Ned drove back to London to work the next day. Since then Ned and Kay toured England with their short breaks away.

After a year of travelling and meeting on a monthly basis Ned and Kay talked about their relationship and agreed that their relationship was surviving with the long distance. After thinking about it for a long time one evening Ned called Kay. "Hello sweetheart, how are you today?" asked Ned. "I feel great and how about you?" asked Kay. Ned was very relaxed and in bed so he gently and in a soft voice replied "I am fine. No change in my life as usual. I am happy having you and look forward to see you next time". "I look forward to see you too, darling", said Kay. "I have an idea and I was wondering if you are in a mood to discuss something that has been in my mind for some time", suggested Ned. "You know I do not like complicated things. If it is simple then go ahead. I am all ears", replied Kay. "I have been thinking about our long distance relationship and ..." was saying Ned when Kay interfered and asked, "you are not thinking about terminating our relationship, are you?". "No, not at all. What do you think I was going to say", asked Ned. "I thought that because of the distance may be you want to finish it. I mean I would understand if you did. Just know that we would always be friends" said Kay. Ned could not believe what he was hearing. Kay was not bothered whether it carried on or finished. But again he was determined to put his idea forward and pointed, "I love you and I would not do that for as long as you do not decide to do so". "Well, I am happy with you at the moment and splitting has not crossed my mind as yet. So what was the idea that you wanted to discuss?", asked Kay. "Last time we agreed that our relationship was going on well, so I was thinking if you would like to come to work in London. We could perhaps share a flat together or if you do not want to share a flat with me and want your own space we could live near each other", suggested Ned. "Right. Carry on. I am listening", said Kay. "I have good contacts in the community and I could get you a job easily or any other jobs you like with good pay. How about that?", suggested Ned. "Sounds good so far", said Kay. She did not say yes and she did not say no. But as she said 'sounds good so far' Ned thought that the answer was positive. So with all excitement he said, "great I will start working on it and see how I get on". "Okay darling. So how is your work going at the moment?", asked Kay and they talked about their work and usual life routine. Ned was so pleased he could not believe his ears. After speaking with Kay he went to bed cheerful. Kay on the other side, after speaking to Ned, went out late to the club with her friends. She was relaxed about the chat and did not think twice about it and did not talk about it to anyone else.

The next morning Ned went to work very excited and made few calls. As there were shortages of nurses in London and nationwide his contacts made a deal for a job. He got appointments for a first meeting and then future interview dates. Kay was about to get her job of her dream and with good conditions and pay. That aspects sorted out, he set off to look for a big one bedroom flat. It took him about a week to find one and got dates to move in. Everything arranged he told Kay about what he had done so far. Kay did not object to anything. So after three weeks Ned moved in the flat and decorated it expertly and got some beautiful furniture. He made the flat very attractive. When everything was sorted out Kay called Ned and they agreed on a date when she would come and visit the flat and know the area prior to attending the meetings. Ned was excited as Kay was coming for a long weekend. They spoke on the phone every night and sent each other cards and little presents.

The night before Kay called and they arranged to meet up at the train station in London. Kay did not want Ned to pick her up. The reason was unknown but Ned did not mind as she was going to stay from Friday until Monday morning. Kay wanted to visit few places in London and wanted to go shopping in Harrods specially. So it was all planned.

23

All excited Ned went to pick Kay up at the station. As usual they were delighted to see each other. They missed the hugging and kissing just as much as the company. They travelled back to the flat. It was on the second floor. So they dragged the luggage and then Ned wanted to surprise Kay. So he asked her to close her eyes while he opened the door. She was there at the doorstep waiting patiently with all excitement. Ned pulled all her personal stuffs in first and then asked Kay to open her eyes. "Wow, it is so beautiful", screamed Kay. She stared at the flat with all amazement. "Did you do it all by yourself?", asked Kay with the eyes wide open. "Yes I did. For you, as you know, I would do anything", replied Ned. Kay was really stunned. She went to the bathroom and the kitchen and looked around. "You turned this flat into a luxury flat. I am delighted to be here. I like it", said Kay. "I hoped you would", said Ned. "We have to celebrate tonight", suggested Kay. "Celebrate, we will. I have champagne ready for tonight. I will make you the best meal. It is a surprise. I know you will like it", said Ned. To that, Kay kissed Ned and then they sat on the king size bed. Kay was mute with amazement. She looked at Ned with tears in her eyes and said, "you did all this for me. I cannot find words to say thank you". Ned did not say anything, as Kay was a bit emotional at the time. After lying down in bed for few minutes they had a cup of tea and then Kay unpacked. She had lots of space in the wardrobe to place her belongings. She had more space that she ever had even in her home at her parents. So she settled after a long and restful bath. Meanwhile Ned was in the kitchen preparing the dinner he promised. Kay got ready and Ned put the dinner in the oven for slow cooking and then they went for a long walk. Ned showed Kay the area he lived in and the facilities around. They also walked to the park and sat down on the grass for a while; talking and sharing the moments they missed while away from each other. They walked back after two hours. Kay opened a bottle of wine and she had some while reading the newspaper. "This is luxury", she said to Ned, "I have not had such a beautiful day for a long time". "Enjoy it and there are many more to come", said Ned all satisfied. He made several trips to the kitchen to check his cooking. It was all done by 6 pm. So he left it in the oven just hot enough to keep it going until they were ready for supper.

Ned went to the bathroom and set everything up for a bath. There was the champagne with two glasses, candles, aromatic oil burning, bath full of bubbles and two silk dressing gown. When it was all ready he went and called Kay. Although she already had a bath Ned asked her to join him in the bath. She left her wine glass, and got in the bathroom. She was amazed. She gently slipped out of her clothing, threw them on the floor and joined Ned who was already in the bath. She slipped in the water and Ned poured the champagne.

"Very romantic", said Kay and she gave Ned a long French kiss. They settled in the bath sipping their champagne. They took all the time in the world. There were no worries about anything, no parents around, no work for few days, just Ned and Kay and free time. They kissed and cuddled in the bath and drunk their champagne. The candles were burning and the aromatic smell in the environment was just out of this world. They relaxed for a long time and then they had sex in the bath. There were no worries about the water splashing. Sex was slow and time consuming. There were no waves, just gentle movement, with long kisses and passion at its best. They had orgasm together. After orgasm, they stayed in the same position for a long time enjoying the after effect and touching each other. "It was beautiful", said Kay. "Yes, it was, darling", commented Ned. And they stayed there for another few minutes.

They then got out and Kay went to the bedroom to dry her hair whilst Ned set the table in the dining room. He was quick as everything was prepared well in advance. By the time Kay came out of the bedroom it was all there. She looked at the room and then looked at Ned who was at the stereo choosing the music. "You are unbelievable", said Kay, "candle lit dinner, with expensive wine, my favourite meal (chicken biryani), and all". Ned smiled and put the music on and came to Kay. He guided Kay to her seat and then he sat down. He served Kay and then himself. They ate and talked. After eating, Ned asked Kay for a slow dance and they danced away until late the night. They went to bed late after having few more glasses of wine. Mixing champagne and wine got them drunk and they slept soundly.

The next morning Ned called his contacts about the job and made appointments for informal visits while Kay was getting ready to go out. They left the flat and went for their appointment as planned. Kay showed great interest and asked many questions to satisfaction. All appointments she attended to were good for her. After that they went to central London for shopping and touring. They walked up to Parliament, Buckingham Palace, Harrods, Trafalgar Square, Leicester Square and then they went to Soho for a Chinese meal. They had a great day in London. They then went to the Cinema in Leicester Square. They returned home late with lots of small bags. They got in very tired. Straight away Ned ran the bath and they got in and relaxed with a glass of wine each. They talked about their day and revived the affectionate moments. Afterwards, they were in bed resting and then Ned asked, " I know it is too soon to ask, but, what do you think of the informal visits?". "It was very generous. Your friends are pleasant", replied Kay. "I mean, which one do you prefer out of curiosity?", asked Ned. "Rewarding jobs. I like them", replied Kay. Ned was tempted to change the subjects as Kay was clearly not giving him any answers. She was very short and was skilfully avoiding the answers Ned wanted to hear. But Ned was not giving up as he was interested to know Kay's decision about the job. So, he asked, "I mean which offer would you accept if you had the choice". Ned hit the nail on the head and was hoping to get a reply. To this question Kay sat in bed and looked away and said, "as you are not giving up I hate to tell you that I will choose not to work in London". She could not face Ned with her answer. She was calm and collective and her voice was low. There was silence. The atmosphere was cutting. Kay did not know what to expect next. Ned was in shock; he did not know what to say. His dream got shattered in seconds. The little moment of silence brought an air of mistrust. He worked hard to get contacts for job, he did his best to get an expensive but affordable flat, he decorated it to Kay's liking, and spent the most wonderful night in his life with the woman he loved. All his emotional investment was going down the drain. "I am sorry if I disappointed you. I know I should have told you earlier but you were so excited about everything that I did not have the gut to stop you. I am sorry. I led you astray. I would understand if you would want to break the relationship", said Kay very gently. Ned was in shock but he knew he loved her and the slight talk or suggestion of breaking up turned his stomach. "I am very disappointed... I am in fact disgusted with the way you handled it... I did everything for nothing... You could have told me, wrote to me or left me a message... anything... I just would have liked to know it before... Can I ask you why?... if I can ask of course", asked Ned. Kay was in tears as usual. She was still looking away with her face very red with embarrassment. "I am sorry Ned. I am fond of you but I love my Dad", said Kay. Ned was quiet. He had to think about his next item of conversation. He was trying to keep calm. He did not want to upset Kay anymore than she was although he was very annoyed. But he was a gentleman who was in love with a beautiful woman. He did not want to lose Kay. So, he said, "I understand that you do not love me anymore. That is clear, as you love your father. I can cope with that. I do not mind for as long as we are together. But as you said earlier if I wish to finish our relationship, it is okay with you, well; I do not want to end our relationship. If you want to then you have to tell me. I will accept your wish. However, I can carry on seeing you as we have been for so long". Ned did not mean what he said from his heart. He was reluctant as he felt that the relationship was not worth keeping alive but he had to see if Kay would end it. After Ned said that Kay turned around and kissed him and put her head on Ned's chest. "I want to keep seeing you. It is far away but I will survive. I am sorry", said Kay. "Okay then in that case there is nothing else to discuss. Let change the mood and have some more wine", suggested Ned. Kay jumped and went to get the wine. Ned and Kay drank the wine and talked about politics. Every time Kay asked a question she could not get a straight reply, as Ned was somewhere else in his mind. He was in deep thought. Thinking about what Shah told him. He was unhappy but love made him blind. He was good and supportive to Kay all the time that he had known her and he was thinking about her behaviour and selfishness towards him. He was so paralysed with her love that he could not even shout or get angry at her. His emotional expression could only show love and, anger, he bottled it up. No one could imagine how disappointed and upset he was but he was continuing to be good to Kay. Anyone else would have flipped by then. After lack of interest from Ned, Kay fell asleep. Ned was still thinking. He could not sleep. It was the first night ever that he was sleeping next to Kay without sex. He sat on the bed with his eyes closed and his head down. He turned round and stared at Kay sleeping. He could not believe how peaceful she looked although she had unstabilised his emotions. He got up and walked around and stood in the bathroom and looked himself in the mirror for along time. After a long while he went to bed and thought that he was going to stay with Kay until he is sure there was nothing left to save in their relationship. So he cleared his mind and fell asleep.

Next morning Kay and Ned stayed in bed till late. Ned was not motivated to do anything. He was not going to make an effort either. Kay as usual expected Ned to get up first and make tea. But Ned was just not in the mood to be considerate and treat Kay as he always did. He gave her everything she asked for and put her first before anyone else and himself. And then that was the result. Ned was quiet in bed with his eyes wide open. Kay asked, "are you alright darling?". After all whatever happened did not mean anything to Kay. She did not even consider how hurt Ned was and then she was asking how he was. Ned lay in bed and looked at her. He already decided what to do in this relationship but he did not know what to say because whatever he would say at that time would be poisonous. On one hand he loved her dearly, on the other he felt betrayed. It was nothing that he did not know and thought about the past. What's next on the menu in the user and abuser section?. After a long pause, "I am fine my dear, just fine … could not feel any better. I feel light and wonderful especially that you are here with me … next to me. Nothing could make me any happier", replied Ned. Kay did not pay much attention to Ned's answer. She was busy preparing herself for the day. Was she bothered, who knew but herself?

"Thank you darling. I know how much you wanted me to be here. But here I am, just here especially for you", said Kay very relaxed. She lay her head on Ned's chest and said, "I love you so much it is unbelievable. I missed you very much". "I thought you were fond of me but love... I think you have to think what you are saying... the meaning of love I know and I can lecture you about it... do you want the lecture?", said Ned. By saying that he wanted Kay to say yes and he was ready to open his heart and say all he wanted to say. But Kay was very diplomatic. She escaped the subject and asked Ned to make a hot cup of tea and they would talk about it then. "And what else do you want with your tea?" asked Ned knowing that the subject about love was closed. "Anything you have on offer, darling", replied Kay. "Tea and sex as usual I suppose", offered Ned. "As you wish, darling", said Kay. But Ned was in no mood for anything. He was trying hard to keep his sanity. He could not understand how Kay could not see what she had done and was happy to continue as usual, business as usual. Ned was being careful in what he was saying, as he did not want to break the relationship as he knew and felt that Kay was trying for Ned to finish the relationship on her behalf. She would not end it as there was no reason for her to end it but she gave Ned plenty of reasons but he was not falling for it. He was being very stubborn. He was in a situation where he could not talk about it to anybody as he did not like being laughed at. So he calmed himself down and decided that he would not be taken for a ride anymore and he would try again. He worked on himself and said, "I am very tired you know. I had a great night sleep but it was not enough. How about you making me a cup of tea for a change?". Kay was shocked. A very simple answer but it was surprising to Kay as Ned never said that to her before. "If you really want me to make it I would … for you", replied Kay shockingly. Ned was pleased that he could stay in bed longer but Kay was not. She went to the kitchen and came back. "I cannot find anything, love. Can you show me where the things are?" asked Kay. "Isn't that funny? The kitchen is small and everything is labelled yet you cannot see the tea bags on the table and the kettle on the table and the milk in the fridge. How nice!", replied Ned. "I just like it when you make it for me, it taste nice. You know!", said Kay lovingly. "Of course, I know", replied Ned. Kay lay down in bed and Ned got up. He was determined not to be used again for the rest of his life, neither by Kay nor by any other living being. So he went to the kitchen and had a glass of water while Kay was waiting for her tea. After that he went to the bathroom and got washed. He came to the bedroom looking fresh and started getting ready for the day. "I am looking forward to my tea", said Kay in a convincing and loving voice. "Me too, but I am going to get mine in the café if you want to join me", said Ned invitingly. He could not make tea for himself and not offer Kay one as this would be rude, and rude he was not. So, hearing Ned's reply Kay jumped off the bed and went to the bathroom and got ready quickly as she knew that Ned would not wait for her. While Ned was on the phone with his contacts cancelling interviews Kay was ready on time. Ned was annoyed as he had to be apologetic on the phone and thanked them for the time and trouble they had gone through to arrange the visits and interviews. Kay could hear his conversation on the phone but she was not the least bothered. After cancelling everything Ned asked Kay to join him for the tea. They left the flat and took a relaxing and easy walk to the café. They still held to their hands and waist as normal. They sat in the café and ordered their tea and breakfast. Ned had two eggs on toast and beans and Kay had two fried eggs on toast. They ate and enjoyed it. They talked about other things of no value, like the transport mess in London and the one-way systems but nothing personal. They were not quiet at any given minute. To Ned that was rubbish talk but he was ready to talk about whatever Kay started. Ned asked for the bill. The bill came and Ned put his hands in his pocket and took out £3.00 and put on the table. He had never done that before with Kay until their short breaks. He had always paid for all her expenses. Kay looked at him and looked at how much he put on the table and realised that she had to pay the other half. Ned was not pleased with what he had done but he had no choice and he did not want to be taken for a ride. Kay put her half and the bill was paid. Kay said nothing. Now the conflict was of a very quiet nature. Half and half and the next step was to be seen. "Breakfast was delicious; I do not mind coming here every morning. Are we going to central London today, darling?", asked Kay. "I think I told you I feel tired today. I mean, just because I am tired does not mean that you have to stay in the flat with me you know. You can by all means go and do whatever you want to do and I will wait for you at home", said Ned. "I would not do that to you. I will stay with you. I will give you a massage and then you will feel better. Perhaps, we could go out at night if you feel rested", suggested Kay. "May be, I don't know how I would feel by then. It is okay, you go … I cannot give you a guarantee that I will go later", said Ned. "I don't mind. If you can, fine. If you cannot, I will still enjoy your company", said Kay. So they walked to that flat and Ned stayed in bed. Kay was reading some woman magazine that she brought from home. While in bed Ned thought that it was not good taking revenge and hurting Kay. There was no point being awkward although he was upset. He had a good thought about the whole thing and decided that he would not be used but he would not get himself bored either. So, he got up and said, "I feel better now. Lets go out and do something", suggested Ned. "That would be nice, darling. As you are making this special effort for me, all expenses are on me, how is that?", said Kay happily. "That's nice Kay, but you know that I will not agree to that. I will pay my share otherwise I will not go", replied Ned. "Okay. Whatever makes you happy", said Kay and they got ready and went out. They walked around and visited few places of interest and in the evening they went to a steakhouse. They enjoyed their meal and walked back home. Ned was quite relaxed and came to terms with what happened. He was ready to continue with the relationship in a different level with a different approach but he was not going to forget what happened so soon. It all depended on Kay whether she would be able to cope with the new approach. Ned was not going to tell Kay anything and he would just change on the way as life went on. They went to that flat and as they were both merry with their drinks they ended up having sex and fell asleep in each other's arms.

The day after Kay got up very early and Ned accompanied her to the station. They waved good-bye and as usual missed each other very much when they were separating. Kay was very sad on the train but pleased that she saw Ned and the flat and where he lived and how he lived. Also she had done her shopping and bought few tokens for her parents and sister. Ned came back to the flat by train and when he got in he dropped himself heavily in bed. He was confused, and unhappy and angry and depressed but he loved Kay and he missed her very much.

Despite all situations, Ned was constantly thinking of Kay in a very positive way. He was angry and upset but then he thought of calling her at night when she was rested from her travel. On the other side Kay got back home and settled in her routine and went to visit her friends in the evening as usual. Her parents did not query much about what she had been up to, as they knew they could trust her with her actions and decisions. At 10.00 in the night Ned called Kay at home. "Hello, it's Ned. Is it possible to speak to Kay please?", asked Ned. Kay's mum answered the call. "Sorry Ned Kay has gone out for the evening. Can I take a message?", asked Kay's mum. "It's okay. I will call later", said Ned. "She might be late. I will tell her that you called anyway", said her mum. "Okay. Thank you", said Ned. Ned was not sure. Kay, under normal circumstances would be tired after the journey back from London and her usual sorting out of things. But he thought it could be that she needed some time out before she got back to work. That night Ned waited for Kay's call until 2.00 in the morning. Still nothing then he fell asleep. He was surprised that Kay did not call back or may be her mum did not given her the message. In the morning Ned called at 11.00 and Kay was not in. Her mum's answer was the same. Very coldly she told Ned that she was not in and that she would leave a message. Ned gave up after that call and waited for a call back whenever it would be. Meanwhile he was getting busy with his work and getting involved in other small businesses with work colleagues. He thought about Kay every day and night and waited for the call.

24

Finally, Kay called two weeks later. Ned answered the phone at midnight. "Hello. Who is it?", asked Ned when he answered the call. "It's me darling", answered the sweet voice of Kay. Hearing Kay, Ned jumped out of bed. He sat on the floor to keep himself awake. "How are you?", asked Ned. "I am great. I am busy lately and out with friends almost every night, you know. Catching up really. And how about you?", asked Kay. "I have been busy but mostly I have been waiting for your call", replied Ned. "How sweet. You are such a darling. I missed you too you know. So when are we meeting again?", asked Kay. Kay was natural. She got away from the subject swiftly and she knew that Ned would always take the opportunity to come and see her. "I would love that. So when is it convenient? I know you seem to be very busy in your social life these days", said Ned. "Now, now, now... don't be like that. There is no reason to be sarcastic. When you come you will see how much I missed you!", said Kay. "In that case you tell me a date from which you can have few days away. A date that will not be changed under any circumstances as I will take days off as well... then we could go to Fort William in Scotland for some special time together", suggested Ned. "That sounds great. I have never been there. I have heard it is a romantic place and Ben Nevis is nearby. We could go on the cable car", said Kay. "Yeah... so let me know. I will be waiting for the dates to negotiate time off at work", said Ned. "Okay. I miss you very much darling. I will call you as soon as I can", said Kay. "Okay then I will wait for your call. I hope it will not be another two weeks", said Ned. Kay laughed and they put the phone down. Ned was satisfied with the conversation and felt better. He took his road map in the middle of the night and looked the road up and the places to visit. He went to bed very late and again he waited for the call from Kay. This time he was not going to call and leave messages. Meanwhile Kay was, as usual, very busy with her friends and her social life. She got a job as nurse in the local hospital and met new people and made new friends. She had an active social life and she had no time to call Ned. So after three weeks Ned sent Kay a post card in an envelope. In the post card he wrote…

"Dear Kay,
It looks like you are very busy. I understand, as I am busy too. However, with difficulty, our relationship as survived with the distance. I do not want to pressure you as I believe in freedom. And love can only progress and develop through freedom and personal space. So when you are free and happen to have some time please call me to let me know of your plans as I do not want to be hanging in the middle. If you make it clear then I can move on and you can move on. I love you dearly and although I know that there is no us and

will never be an 'us' I hope that we will be able to have a mutually agreeable relationship. Thinking of you.
>
> Yours,
>
> Ned."

The letter was very short and to the point. The next day Kay called. "Hello Ned. I got your letter. It was a beautiful surprise to hear from you. Sorry I cannot be long on the phone as I am on a pay phone away from home. I will call you as soon as I get back home", said Kay quickly. After that her cash ran out and that was it. Ned did not have time to say anything, not even hello! But then he thought if she was away how comes she knew about the letter. Her conversation was very short and that meant that she had not read it. It also meant that her parents told her that there was a letter from London and that could only be Ned. So Ned thought when Kay got back home and read the letter then she would call. The story was exactly as he assumed and predicted. She was away with her so-called friends and she did not even bother calling Ned about their short holiday together. She was busy with work and all. So Ned was as usual waiting. Ned was the trusting type and in the nurses home they always trusted each other, and they were never jealous from whatever the other did because they knew that they loved one another. So, Ned was not bothered about her friends and their activities; Kay was quite content with Ned although their time apart was getting longer and longer. Kay knew that Ned would not be unfaithful to her and Ned was faithful too. So he went to work and went to the pub with colleagues after work. Meanwhile, Kay was busy with her work and social life. It was two weeks since the previous short call from the phone box.

It was midnight again when the phone rang. Ned was deep asleep and was awaken by the rings. He picked up the phone and sleepily answered the call. He was expecting it to be Kay as it was late but then she had been busy. "Hello", answered Ned. "Hello darling it's meeeee...", said Kay all excited. That was quite a shock. In the middle of the night she was calling with all excitement. "What's up? You seem very excited", said Ned. "Well, should I not call you? It is exciting calling you. I hope it is for you too!", said Kay. "Of course it is pleasing to hear from you. So what is the plan?", asked Ned hoping that Kay had read the letter. "Nothing much. As usual. Life goes on you know", replied Kay. Ned was not the inquisitive type and he was not going to ask what she had been up to and where she went because he simply would not interfere. "So, I take it that you have not thought about what I asked in the letter", commented Ned. "I thought I replied to your question. I said that there was nothing much and business as usual. So I am ready to carry on as we are. We have quality time together. I feel that it is good to have short times together than lots of long and boring time. And we have quality short times together which seems good so far. I hope it is okay with you", said Kay. "I have no problem with that for as long as it is okay with you. But it seems to me that our times apart are getting longer and longer and the phone contacts are getting rare and in the middle of the night", asserted Ned. "I am sorry darling. You know how it is working shifts and then coming at home and doing things and then time just disappears in a blink but I will try to call more often", said Kay. "Okay. Do not worry about it. What about our short break in Fort William?", asked Ned. "Great. Now you are talking. That's what I called you for. I have negotiated time off but the only problem is that it will be in six weeks", replied Kay. "What? That makes two and a half months without seeing you!!", shouted Ned. "I mean I am trying my best here, you know", said Kay. "Okay then give me the dates... how about meeting in the middle for a day or an evening for dinner?", suggested Ned. "Well, I have to work and put in the hours to get those days off to go away. So I will be working everyday. And it is not worth it for you to come all the way just for few hours. I would not do that to you", said Kay. "I don't mind. Think about it", said Ned and then they exchanged the dates and times for meeting and leaving for Fort William. Kay also gave Ned the assurance that she would call him more regularly and that she would return his calls.

So she did. They spoke twice a week on a regular basis. During their chats Kay asked Ned to come for the dinner as he suggested previously as she was getting frisky and Ned was getting very hot. Three weeks later Ned drove to Kay's home on a Friday afternoon. This time he had his new fast and racy car. It was a pleasant drive and speeding on the motorway in a new car was great. He arrived at Kay's at 7.00 in the evening. When he got there he had a warm welcome. Ned was in his best suit and her parents were rather shocked and he got a lot of compliments. It was unusual but the compliments were taken. He was waiting for Kay to come down. Meanwhile her parents and sisters were entertaining him with tea and cakes and were friendly. It seemed strange to Ned. After 20 minutes Kay came down looking radiant in her best evening dress. She came and kissed Ned in front of her parents and they went out straight away. Her parents and sister looked at them going out to dinner and waved at them from the door just like in the movies and shouted at them "have a nice time" and all. So they left. They went to a top restaurant for steak. Ned liked steak and Kay loved it too. Could not be better. Ned drove Kay and she looked very proud to travel in his posh car. In the car they talked and laughed and everything was normal. They got in the restaurant and received first class service. The meal was great. After the restaurant they went to a pub where Kay used to go with her friends. She was a regular there so the landlord knew her. They had a warm welcome there. After an hour of being there, half an hour before closing time came Kay's friends. They did not know anything about Ned. So Kay introduced Ned as her best friend from London. They all sat there and had a good chat and a good time. From there Kay wanted to take a cab home as Ned had to go a long way but Ned would not have it. And Kay resumed to the idea for Ned to drop her home. They had more drinks and then Ned took her home. By the time they got there they were both hot and steamy. Kay opened the door gently and they got in the kitchen. Little did she know that her parents were awake and waiting for her? Kay and Ned got engaged in a very hot and steamy sex. Dress and suit were flying everywhere in the kitchen and they had sex on the dinner table. It was great. They loved it and enjoyed every moment of it. However, her parents could hear everything as their bedroom was above the kitchen. Ned and Kay did not think about it as it was late and they were merry and joyful. After sex they got dressed and sat in the lounge until Ned was fit to drive. At 3.00 in the morning, after few coffees they had more sex and then Ned left. Meanwhile Kay's parents were whispering to one another. They knew what happened but they were not going to talk about it to Kay. They were a bit confused as Kay was going out regularly with colleagues and yet she was having sex with Ned. They were worried and uncertain about the future. They also knew that Ned and Kay were going away for few days and that did not please them very much but they did not have much choice. If they were to keep their daughter they had to keep quiet and try not to put fuel to the fire.

That night was wonderful for Kay. Ned went home happy and Kay went to bed. Kay kept busy with her side of the world and Ned on his side of life. They spoke regularly until they had to go to Scotland.

25

Nearer the time Ned and Kay discussed their meeting and preparation about going to Fort William for few days. As planned Ned went to Kay's home to pick her up for the break. This time her parents received him even better than last time. It was rather confusing for Ned because they did not want Kay to have anything to do with him yet they were improving in their interpersonal relationship. He tried not to think about it too much and he did not want to make an issue of it as it was in his advantage. The days of sarcasm and hatred have gone and they had moved on. So that was good or wasn't it? As usual Kay was late getting ready and packed. Her dad helped her to get all the luggage down and they gave the spare duvets and pillows just in case they could not find a bed and breakfast and they had to rent a caravan or sleep in the car. They made good preparation and her father had good advice for Kay in case they got stuck. Kay's father took the car keys off Ned while he was having tea and loaded the car. He also checked the oil and water levels and the brake fluid. How nice? But on the other hand he was only taking care of his daughter. All set Kay got in the car with Ned and they left. It was a long drive from where Kay lived. They made two comfort stops and had snacks and continued their journey until they reached their destination. Once there, they were quick getting B&B. So easy as Ned was in demand because of his colour. He did not know that Scottish people liked the fair colour and foreigners. He did not mind as he was the centre of attention. He was warmly welcomed in the B&B. They settled in and looked at some of the leaflets they picked up at the tourist information centre. It was all great. They had a rest and settled down with a glass of wine. Ned was tired from all the driving and he fell asleep with the newspaper and the wine. Kay lay down and relaxed with her woman's magazine.

By the evening they both got up and got ready to go out for dinner. They went for a pizza and afterward they went to the pub nearby for a drink. They had a relaxing time and there was no interest for sex that night. They just cuddled up and went to sleep. They needed a good rest as the next day they were going to Ben Nevis.

The following morning they got up at 11.00. They were late for breakfast as normally it finished at 9.30 am. So they got ready and went downstairs. They were not expecting anything. They sat down and looked at the papers and other leaflets for touring. During that time the landlady came and offered them tea. They did not refuse although they already had tea in their room. After serving them tea the landlady called them in the dining room and served them with breakfast. Both Ned and Kay could not believe it. The landlady was friendly and very chatty (not too much). She also talked to them about places in the vicinity to visit. She was glad to have Ned in her building as he was supposed to bring luck. They got to know each other very well. She also offered to make supper for them, free of charge. However, after a late breakfast Ned and Kay drove to Ben Nevis. Once there they took a cable car and went of the peak. They stayed there and walked around and took pictures. They had tea and cakes in the café and then came down. It was beautiful and it was packed with tourists. They then went to the natural sites and spent time in the wild. They got back around 7.00 in the evening. The landlady made them steak and chips with vegetables. Dinner was delicious indeed. They stayed down and chatted about the culture and Ned tried the kilt. It was funny with Ned in a kilt without underwear but it was good experience. Afterwards Kay and Ned went to their room, relaxed and cheerful. After refreshing themselves they watched television in the company of a glass of wine. It was luxury. No work, no pressure, Kay was next to Ned, there were no phone calls, no parents to tell them what to do and no disturbance. It was just two of them in their company.

After couple glass of wine and they got very frisky. They started kissing and fondling each other. All detailed action was taken to its maximum, as they were very comfortable in the environment. They explored their sexual fantasies and then resumed to penetrative sex. Ned penetrated and stopped and pulled back out. "What is the matter? Anything wrong?", asked Kay. "Not really it just feels very different", replied Ned. "What do you mean?", questioned Kay. "I don't know. It is just different", replied Ned. "Well I do not think it is different. The only thing is that my period is late by four days. Normally it is like the clockwork", said Kay.

"May be that's what it is", said Ned. And they continued with their passion. This sex session was the longest ever. Kay's was more passionate then ever. She just was not having enough and wanted more and more, and so they did until late at night and very early hours on the morning. After that they collapsed in bed.

The next morning they got up, had breakfast and went for a long drive to Joan-a-Groats, the top end of Scotland. Ned wanted to go there desperately as he heard that it was a sight not to be missed. And also that meant that he had driven the full length of the United Kingdom, from Lands End to the top. They went there and as it was such a beautiful place they stayed there and sat on the cliffs for a long time enjoying the view and the different types of birds flying around. It was just out of this world as Kay put it. They sat there and day dreamed in the splendid weather. From there they came back to their B&B and had another dinner. They had a drink with the landlady and then went upstairs. After refreshing themselves Ned asked Kay to lie down next to him in bed. He raised her dressing gown and gently put his hands on her belly. "What are you looking for darling?", asked Kay. "I am concerned. You look a bit different and I do not think it is just because of delayed period!", said Ned. "I do not feel any different than before", said Kay. "Kay, are you very sure there is nothing developing inside?", asked Ned worryingly. "I am one hundred and ten percent positive. If there was anything I should be the first one to feel it. It is just delayed period all from being busy and stressed lately. There is nothing to worry about darling", replied Kay reassuringly. Kay comforted, and reassured Ned and then they settled down and had another passionate evening. However, after sex Ned was still not convinced that everything was okay but he was not going to say anything and ruin the holiday. He was certain about his assumption as sex was slightly different although more exciting and wild. So he fell asleep thinking about it. There was no issue made the next morning. They went to Isle of Skye to see sea lions. It was a beautiful day and they had a small picnic with them. They enjoyed the time they had together. On the way back they stopped by an Indian restaurant and had a delicious meal. Everywhere they went they made friends and exchanged addresses. Kay and Ned seemed to attract attention due to their mixed race relationship. They got back to the B&B and went straight to their room, as the landlady was not in. They watched television and drank wine. They chatted and life could not be anymore beautiful for both of them. They decided that it was better to have quality few days together than a lot of few hours together. They decided that they would meet as often as time allowed and have similar times away from everyone and work and enjoy life. Kay and Ned were at ease with this idea as they felt rested and could enjoy each other's company better. They could talk and just be there for each other. That night there was no sex as they were quite happy talking. They were surprised when they looked at the time. 4.00 in the morning and they were still talking. They slept after that as they intended to go to Oban the next day. And so they did after waking up late. As before the landlady was there for them and made them homemade brunch and gave them some food for the road. She was kind and motherly. They drove to Oban and visited some natural spots and they took a leisurely drive back to

Fort Willaim. They had enjoyable days. They were not bored for a single minute. Kay was content and Ned was happy. They got back to the B&B and had a special candle-lit dinner made for them. They enjoyed every bite of it and they settled in bed. Needless to say that they had a great night, and passion was their surname. Late in the night just before going to sleep Kay was in tears as it was their last night together and she enjoyed it so much. She was going to miss Ned a lot and that made her emotional. She held on to Ned and fell asleep. Ned was satisfied with Kay and he came to terms with what happened with the idea of staying in London with Kay and accepted the situation as it was. He was more settled and contented with the new development and progress of their relationship. He came to terms with it but he was not forgetting it. For Ned, life was like driving a car, 'drive forward but keep looking in the rear mirror', to be a little bit more careful.

They had a good rest and the next day they woke up at 10.00 in the morning. They got ready and went down for breakfast. The landlady was there. She already packed them up with lunch and snacks for the way. She made a very…very…very big breakfast. Ned thought they were never going to eat that amount but surprisingly they did. It was light and delicious. When they finished they loaded the car and then both Ned and Kay went back in to pay. "Jane, it is time to say good-bye. And I would like to settle the bill", said Ned. "It is ready. One minute and I will bring it", said Jane. She went in the kitchen and brought the bill. Ned looked at it and then gave it to Kay to look at it. "That cannot be right", commented Ned. Jane looked offended by this comment. "I hope it is not too expensive", said Jane. Kay was in the middle and looking. She was shocked. "I am sorry Jane but I cannot pay you this sum. You did a lot for us and the meals are not included. I can't do that. Please put the price of the dinners and the pic-nic on top of the room price ... please", asserted Ned. "Ned, you are a gentleman. And even more so you are a good man and a genuine man. I hope Kay will appreciate you. Kay is a lucky girl to have someone like you. What I did was as a token of friendship. I wanted Kay and you to have a good rest and enjoy your time. For me, when I see both of you being over the moon it is enough. I normally get clients who would not even bother to talk or have a decent conversation. It has been a pleasure having you", said Jane. "Ned was embarrassed and would not budge without paying more than what Jane billed. So he gave Jane the payment and put £20.00 in the charity box at the entrance. Ned could not believe of the hospitality from someone he hardly knew. They said their good-byes and exchanged phone numbers and addresses for Christmas cards. After settling everything Kay and Ned came to the car and Jane followed. "It is lucky to have a coloured person in the house. Come during New Year. I will treat you to a complimentary stay", said Jane. "I will try, thank you Jane", said Ned. Jane approached Ned and gave him a kiss on both cheeks and a hug. Ned then drove off and he could see the landlady looking at them until they were out of sight. "I like Scottish people, I can tell you that. I don't mind being a luxury", commented Ned. "Meanwhile, I have the luxury", said Kay squeezing Ned's hand on the gear stick.

Kay and Ned drove back. Ned dropped Kay at her home and had dinner with her parents. Her mum prepared roast chicken and roast potatoes and broccoli and cauliflower. It was appreciated that her mum took the trouble. They were not the least bothered about them. After dinner Kay got a long list of messages from her friends. "You have been in demand whilst you have been away love. Hope you return your calls as soon as you are refreshed", said Kay's mum. Kay put the paper on the shelf away from the dining table. "Do not worry mum. I will return the calls. For the time being I want to enjoy Ned's company", said Kay to her mum. Her parents left them to continue with their talks. Ned then thanked her parents for the meal and he left after 3 hours. He drove back late at night so that he would not encounter any obstruction on the motorway. They had a great time from beginning to end and Ned was welcome at Kay's house. So it could not get any better. After Ned's departure Kay caught up with her messages. Ned went back to London very tired and went straight to bed.

26

Back in London, Ned got on with his life routine as usual. At her home Kay got in her busy work and social routine as previously. But then on the third night Ned had a dream. He dreamt that he was the father of a baby-boy and that life as a father was beautiful and exciting. The only thing was that he could not see who the mother was in the dream. Kay was not there and he only dreamt of himself playing with the child and feeding him and changing his nappies. He was a lovely child and full of energy and extremely good-looking and attractive. It was a pleasant dream. When Ned got up in the morning he could remember every details of his dream. And he went to work as usual. While working he suddenly realised that Kay was delayed with her period. Suddenly there were lots of issues in his mind, father, unmarried, Kay, Kay's parents, mixed race child, and many 'ifs'. His mind was working overtime at work. He could not concentrate. So, he took the afternoon off and got back home. He had to call Kay but at the same time he had to get it right in his head, all the 'ifs' and 'buts'. As far as he was concerned he had no problem with all the 'ifs and buts' as his parents loved Kay and they already accepted Kay in his family as she was, but what on the other side. Ned spent the whole afternoon in bed thinking. Then he thought there was no point speculating. He had to call Kay to find out what was happening.

He waited until 10 pm. He timed it very well so that he would get Kay on the phone. He gave another half an hour for tea and rest then he called. "Hello", answered Kay's sister. "Hi, it is Ned", said Ned. "It is lovely to hear from you. I heard all about your trip to Scotland from Kay. She really enjoyed it. I would like to go there myself", said Kay's sister. "Yes, it was good. I recommend it. I would like to speak to Kay if she is in", asked Ned. "She just left 15 minutes ago. Can I leave a message for her?" asked Kay's sister. "If you would not mind please ask her to call me urgently as soon as she gets this message", said Ned. "Okay. Will do. I hope you are all right", said Kay's sister. "Yeah, I am fine. Just needed to speak to Kay really", said Ned. "Okay. I will make sure that she gets the message and that she calls you", said her sister. And they hung up. Ned found it a bit odd that her sister was trying to maintain a conversation with him. That had never happened before. However, he could not understand that Kay went out after work. But again she had new friends and was busy. Ned waited for the return call until 2.00 in the morning then he went to bed. He was worried and was paranoid about his dream. Deep down he would have liked to have a child whether boy or girl, it did not matter. But he was worried about Kay.

He called again in the morning before going to work. Her mum answered the call and said that she was not in and that she did not know when she would be back. It was obvious that she did not get the message. So,

Ned went to work. He called again at 2.00 in the afternoon. Her dad answered the phone and he said that Kay came in and went to work in a rush as she was late. Unusual, she would have called him after an urgent message. But again that was Kay she would only call when she would be free to talk. When Kay came back from work, she called Ned at home at 10.00 pm.

"Hello darling. What is the matter? I had so many messages from everyone to call you. Are you alright?", asked Kay directly. "I am fine. Thank you. You seem to have been busy. Can't catch you or catch up with you. Never mind, how are you?", asked Ned. "I feel great, full of energy. I don't know where I get all the energy from!... ... I miss you very much. When am I going to have a good time like Scotland with you?", asked Kay. "Any time you like. We just have to sort the time off and we are off. Just mention where and when and I will take you there", replied Ned. "So what is worrying you Ned. What is in your mind?", asked Kay. "Well, you might say I am paranoid but I have to ask you. Have you had your period yet?", asked Ned. "Oh, I forgot all about it. I did not think about it again since we got back. No I have not had my period yet. I do not feel any different. Why?" asked Kay. "It is just that I had a weird dream. I really would like you to have a pregnancy test", said Ned. "No I am not. It is my body and I know 'me' very well. I am not pregnant!!", said Kay abruptly. "Okay. I understand what you are saying. Why don't you just do a test and it will put my mind to rest. And will save you some hassle. Please", begged Ned. Kay was not at all pleased about this conversation let alone doing the test. She was very annoyed, as she never had this type of dialogue with any previous boyfriends in the past. But then there was no harm trying. It took Ned a lot to convince Kay. He practically begged her to do it. "Okay. I know you are getting annoyed with me. Please do it for me", said Ned. "Okay then I will do it", said Kay. "When?", asked Ned. "Talk about pressurising me!", answered Kay. "Okay, when you are ready. But please let me know straight away what the result is", said Ned. "Alright. I will do it tomorrow. I will call you and do it when you are on the phone with me. Okay? That will put your mind at rest", said Kay. "Okay. Thank you. I am sorry if I make you feel harassed", said Ned. "Don't worry. I know you mean it for the best", said Kay and they talked about other things and they planned their meeting for a short break to Skegness. Kay did not talk about her period during the conversation and Ned did not ask anything else just in case he would aggravate Kay. At least for that time he was pleased that she was going to do the test the next evening. After talking to Kay, Ned went to sleep with his mind at rest. And Kay went out to see her friends.

27

The next day after work she stopped at Superdrug and bought two pregnancy test kits and hid them in her bag. She came home and went straight to her room and hid them in her drawer and locked it so that no one would accidentally see them. After that she had a cup of tea and left to see her friends. She had to meet them at 4.00 in the afternoon. She came back at home at 9.30 pm as she was going to call Ned at 10.00 pm. She had a shower and got ready for bed relaxed and waited patiently to call Ned.

At 10.00 pm sharp, the phone rang. "Hello", answered Ned. "It's only me darling", said Kay. "Are you okay?", asked Ned. "Yeah, just had a very busy day today. I am nervous to do the test", said Kay. "Well, either that or you can back down. Choice is yours", said Ned. "I have got the test kit. I will do it now. It is for the best", said Kay. "Okay I will be on the phone", said Ned. "Okay, I will go and start it", said Kay. While Ned was waiting on the phone Kay went to the bathroom and applied her urine in the square. "It is done. Now we have to wait", said Kay. The test took four minutes. There was a long silence. Ned was worried on his end of the phone and Kay was sweating on the other side.

Ned could hear her heavy breathing on the phone. Kay put the test kit on the bed and looked away and timed four minute on the clock. As soon as the minute hand counted 4 minutes she turned round and looked. Ned on the other side timed his watch as well and just as the four minutes passed away he asked Kay, "so what is it". At the same time Kay's eyes were on the little square. She was fixed on it and the phone dropped. "What's up Kay? Ned was asking from the other end of the line. Meanwhile Kay's whole world turned upside down, the test result was strongly positive. She picked the phone off the floor. "It is positive", said Kay quietly. "Okay", said Ned. There was silence. Kay was numb. Ned was still. "It is not right. I am sure the test result is wrong. I have had quite a bit to drink tonight. I am sure it is wrong", said Kay after a long silence. "I don't think it is wrong Kay", said Ned. "I can't speak to you about this on the phone. How about meeting next week?", suggested Kay. "I do not mind coming tomorrow", replied Ned. "No. No. I am out tomorrow. Come on your next day off. I have to go now just in case someone hears me on the phone", said Kay. Ned quickly looked in his diary and they negotiated a day convenient to both of them. Kay went off line quickly. She did not really want to talk about anything. Ned was accepting and coming to terms with it quickly as he was in doubt from before and his mind got around it quicker. He also thought of all eventualities of 'ifs' and he was ready to be a father and his only concern was the non-acceptance of Kay's parents. But again, he thought he was a good earner and had good future prospects and could afford a child and also buy a house and not only give them a good life but also a luxurious life. He just had to wait for Kay. He did not want to say anything, nothing of what he thought about just in case Kay would get upset. So he waited for the next week patiently. Meanwhile, on the night of the test, after the call Kay counted her period dates. She was late by nearly four weeks. She could not understand how she missed it all that time. She had been so busy she did not have time to think about it. Any other girl with an active sex life would be worried after a week. She went to the bathroom and looked at her belly. It looked different. Her face was a bit swollen and she tried her jeans. They were slightly tight. She got worried. She could not talk about it to anyone and more so not her friends. Everyday she went to work with the thought of a baby in her mind and that she was carrying a human being inside. Every night she continued with her social life and went for meals with friends. Her friends thought that Kay was eating more than usual and jokingly they commented that she was going to expand quickly. Kay's answer was simple, "it is quick to put it on and I can lose it very quick with a strict diet girls. I want to enjoy my dinner". And everything was turned into a joke and a laugh. She was careful as to what she said when she spoke to anyone and was careful with what she wore. It was a nerve wrecking few days until Ned was there. Ned was nervous and had to be careful in handling the situation.

Ned arrived at Kay house on the Friday morning as planned. Kay took the day off and they went for a walk in the local park. They were both quiet and walking slowly. Ned tried to hold Kay's hand but could not as there was a pronounced distance although they were walking close together. They went to the end of the park. "This is where the park ends. What do you want to do", said Kay in a dry tone. "I don't mind walking or sitting down somewhere", replied Ned. "Okay, let's sit down on the bench", suggested Kay. They sat down very close still not holding hands. The feeling between them was uncertain. Kay was looking at the opposite direction to Ned. There were few minutes of silence. "So, have you given some thoughts to the situation?", asked Ned. "I have done nothing else but think about it", replied Kay still looking at the opposite direction. "What is the way forward?", asked Ned. "I don't know", replied Kay. Then she looked at Ned very deeply in his eyes and held his hands. "I can see that you want this child, don't you?", said Kay. Ned was surprised to this comment and did not know what to say. Then after few seconds of looking blank he held tightly to Kay hands. "I believe that whatever happens, happens for a reason. I would love to have a child. But it cannot be my decision only. It is a joint affair", replied Ned. "I knew you wanted it", said Kay with tears in her eyes. She started crying. Ned held on to her tightly and supported her. "I have been good to you until now and I will support you forever. My love for you is forever, you know. Why are you in tears?", asked Ned. "Well…the fact is I have something inside me and there are decisions to be made", said Kay. "My question is, would you go ahead?", asked Ned. "You would like me to, won't you?", replied Kay. "I would because I do not believe in taking life away. But then it is a joint decision", said Ned. "What if I said yes?", asked Kay. Ned looked at Kay and felt hopeful and looked pleased. "Then I would ask you to marry me. Not because you are pregnant but because I love you", replied Ned. "And what if I said no?", asked Kay. Ned went mute following this question. He did not think about that before. "Then I suppose we have to think what the options will be", replied Ned. "Okay. I will not beat about the bush. I have decided and I have made up my mind. There is no time to think about it for a long time and every day that goes by is a day lost", said Kay. Ned was in shock. What next? She had been thinking about it for a long time and then the decision was already made and basically Ned had no say in it. He was not going to fight with Kay over her decision but he was determined to ask her for justification. After all he was the father. "What do you mean?", asked Ned in a very disappointed tone of voice. "I am sure you have guessed by now... I want that thing out of me", Kay said angrily. 'That thing' thought Ned, Kay was not referring to 'the child' or any other words to define what she carrying but 'that thing'. He was disappointed. He knew things would go ape-shape following that conversation. "I want it out of my body", continued Kay. 'That thing', 'it', and what next thought Ned. The expression she used got Ned very annoyed and he decided to ask her few key questions to understand her. May be she was upset, or may be she was blaming Ned for everything. If Kay could explain that then Ned would accept it. "Kay, you know that I love you very much. You know that I would do anything for you. Why do you refer to your pregnancy by 'that thing and it'", asked Ned. "I do not want a baby. What … you want me to give a name to it?", replied Kay. "I understand that you want an abortion, yeah. But can I ask what is wrong about having my child if you love me? It is not about anybody, it is about you and me" said Ned. "I am going to make this very clear and very simple. I have been trying to be polite but I am making it very clear… I do not want a coloured child!!", said Kay. With that answer, Ned's blood pressure went in his boots. In the few seconds that he was quiet his whole world fell apart. His entire investment in this relationship went nil. His love was unreciprocated and he felt used. Used he knew he was but to the extent that he was in disbelief. He was in shock. His eyes were full of tears for the first time in his life. He was numb. All feelings disappeared. He stared at Kay and she was looking back at him. Their hands fell apart. "I hope you are not saying that just to hurt me Kay. I thought you were fond of me and you liked me very much. So much that you would do anything", said Ned carefully without using the word love. "I am not doing this to hurt you. I love my father more than I love you. And under no circumstances will I hurt him. I do not want to lose my father. I love him. I hope you will understand", said Kay. Ned was in no way going to understand that but then the decision was made. Who was he do decide? He had to go with the flow. Kay was cold to him. "Okay. Decision made. Just remember one thing, you are carrying my child and I would like to see you through this no matter how much it hurts me. I just want to make sure that you are all right afterwards", said Ned. "Thank you, darling. I knew you would understand. You are my best chum", said Kay. Ned was angry but he was a gentleman. Any other man would have let the woman go alone and deal with it on her own, but his love for Kay was too strong. He felt stupid being used and now spat at but he was the victim of love. No one normal would put up with that. Even when he was coldly told that Kay loved her father more than she loved him, he was still willing to see her through it. Ned felt helpless. Everything went down the drain. "Okay. What is the next step?", asked Ned unwillingly. "Lets go home and I will call my doctor and make an appointment for this evening. They have late closing time today", suggested Kay. Ned did not reply and Kay stood up and started walking. Ned followed. Kay pulled Ned and held his hands as if there was nothing wrong, as if business as usual. They drove to Kay's home. Kay checked every corner of the house to ensure there was nobody in to hear her conversation on the phone. All checked and doors secured for unexpected visitors she called her doctor. She explained the family doctor the situation in brief and in confidence and asked for an urgent appointment. The doctor explained to her that abortion would be the last option and he had to have both parties, that is, the boyfriend and her there to make a sound decision. Under normal circumstances the doctors did not favour abortion where there was stable relationship. And Kay told the doctor that they had a stable and healthy relationship. So he asked her to bring her boyfriend along. All along the dialogue on the telephone Ned was quiet and listening. He could not believe it was all happening, he just could not believe it. He considered himself very stupid. "How could I be taken for a ride and still be here and take this rubbish. I am not normal", Ned kept repeating to himself. Meanwhile Kay made the appointment and after that they had a cup of tea and sat down. There was complete silence. Whilst they were waiting for the time to pass, Kay was sitting on the armchair and reading the woman's magazine and Ned was holding his head in his hands, looking down to the floor. After two hours of silence they got ready and went to the doctors surgery.

All arrangements were working out well. As far as Kay and Ned knew, the doctor would speak to them together and would make a joint decision regarding the next step. They had already decided what to do, or rather Kay had decided what to do and Ned had no choice but to follow her decision. Ned was not going for another cold war but instead of aggravating the situation he thought of going along with Kay. They got to the doctor's surgery, which was in Kay's village. She had to be careful, as the information would reach her mum quickly. They went in very relaxed and reported to the reception. The doctor was notified and Ned and Kay were asked to sit in the queue. They sat next to one another looking very distant although they would have liked to hold each other. They waited. During that time there were a lot of things that Ned was thinking about: his religious position, his beliefs, his values and how to cope with what was about to happen. Next to him, there was Kay thinking about her whole future, what if the doctor disagreed, what if there was something wrong that would interfere with the abortion, what and what and what? They were both worried. Since Kay already made the decision and Ned already knew that she did not want a mixed race child, let alone a mixed relationship, various feelings about the subject remained undiscussed.

The waiting time seemed long specially especially when the people in the surgery kept staring at Ned as if he just landed from Mars. Then, there was Kay's turn. Her doctor came to get her. She stood up and shook his hand. "Are you alone?" asked the old doctor. At this point Ned stood up. "This is Ned", said Kay. The doctor looked surprised. He gave Ned a look that he was never going to forget. "It's okay, Kay, you can come on your own", said the doctor. Kay was so tense that she did not say anything and just followed the doctor as he asked. Ned was so annoyed that he could get nothing out of his mouth. He suddenly lost all his words. He sat down looking like the biggest fool in the surgery, let alone in town and in his life. All the people in the waiting room were Caucasian and they all looked at him. The on-lookers obviously worked out that they were supposed to go in together and hence there was a relationship. During the time that Kay went in, the people in the waiting room were staring at Ned and whispering to each other. He found it uncomfortable but he had to stay. He did not realise how different the attitude was compared to London and Scotland. May be the people there were out of tune, but then the doctor's behaviour and expression on his face was just unacceptable (to Ned's standard). Few minutes later Kay appeared with a smile. "Let's go Ned", said Kay and she led the way without waiting, as if in a rush. They got out of the surgery and went straight in the car. Ned drove off. "Let's go to a café where we can talk and have a tea. I feel dry", said Kay. "As you wish. I can do with a tea as well. How was it", asked Ned. "It is still sinking in my mind. I will tell you once I have sorted it out in my head", replied Kay. "Okay, in your own time, no pressure", said Ned. Ned did not want to make assumptions anymore. So they went to the nearest café. They took a table aloof. They had their tea and cakes and ordered more tea. "Okay. Are you ready?", asked Kay. "Yeah", said Ned. "It goes like this. My doctor has booked a private clinic outside this area for abortion. It is in two weeks time. The time of the operation is not important and it is a day thing. He booked it over the phone. All confirmed. No letters are expected at home", said Kay all relaxed. "Impressive. That was quick, all in the few minutes you were in. I thought he wanted to talk to me as well but by the look of it my colour made his decision very fast", said Ned in all disappointment. "Now... don't be like that. It is hard already. Yeah... I was disappointed that he asked me to come with him alone. And yes...when he got in he did not ask any question and he was straight on the phone making arrangement. So what? This is what I wanted and to me no matter what the discussion would have been in the doctor's room, my decision would still have been the same", said Kay. "Got it loud and clear. In fact it could not be any clearer", said Ned in a quiet tone. He did not make an issue of it. He was co-operative because there was no room to be uncooperative. They finished the pot of tea in a civilised fashion and left the café with smile on the face. They got in the car. Kay was pleased. She then had to work out how to go about going to the clinic without her parents not knowing anything. "Ned would you come to the clinic with me?", asked Kay. "If that's what you want me to do...", replied Ned. "I feel scared. And I do not want anyone to know where I am going. My parents only allow me to go with you without questions", said Kay. "So tell them that we will be going to Wales for couple of days and I will come to pick you up as usual", said Ned. Decision was made very quickly. "You are a gem. Thank you. I will pay for all expenses", said Kay. "Do not worry about that. We will sort that out afterwards. It is still early, what do you want to do?", asked Ned. "Well. Last few days have been stressful. I want to treat you to a meal", offered Kay. "I like that", said Ned. Kay was happier and more relaxed that things would be sorted out. They drove to the nearest Harvester. They had a steak and had a bottle of wine. They talked and they were both feeling better afterwards. The whole situation changed. They were more normal than two hours ago. Ned settled down and Kay was feeling more human. They talked about their plans to go to "Wales" and how they would meet and what to take. They were going to stay in a hotel for a change so that they would be warm, comfortable and accessible to a doctor should there be any complications afterwards. They decided and planned everything and covered all possible variables so that they would be safe and Kay's parents would not know. They finished their meal and went to the park for a walk. They were feeling frisky after the drinks and ended up having sex in the open air. Then Kay knew that her passion was greater than before and she did not hold herself back with the screams and moaning and groaning in the park. They were tired after a tense day. Ned dropped Kay at home. He did not want to meet her parents, therefore left straight away. While driving there was a lot of things in his mind that he had to come to terms with. He was unhappy with the abortion, what to do next with his relationship, how to live with himself afterwards and his love life altogether. But what affected him most was that Kay was not having a mixed race child and that she loved her dad more than him. He felt used. He knew this was one episode in his life that he would never forget. Ned got back to London and carried on as usual. He went to visit Shah regularly and went to all parties. He got drunk more often than usual. Shah was worried about him but Ned became very closed and Shah could not ask him any personal questions until Ned was ready to open up. But one thing Shah knew for sure was that Ned was not himself and he promised himself to be there for him whenever and wherever needed. Meanwhile Kay lived her life as normal as she could and went out partying every night. She stayed out quite a lot which Ned knew about.

28

Two weeks went very quick. It was time for Ned to be strong and supportive to someone for something that he did not approve of. So he got up early in the morning, earlier than usual to pray. He asked for forgiveness for he was not strong enough to fight for the unborn child and again he had to ask for forgiveness because he had not tried hard for Kay to keep the child. But then it was not his body. So he got his mind sorted out and drove off to Kay. He was there by 7.00 in the morning. He went in. Her parents were waiting with a cup of tea. They had a quick breakfast while Kay's dad loaded the car and they drove off. They were on the road by 7.30 in the morning. They were at the clinic at 11.00am. They registered at the reception. Ned was asked to wait in the waiting room. Kay went in. During the time when Ned was waiting, he prayed that nothing would go wrong and that Kay would be safe and healthy and able to conceive again. He prayed and prayed again and again. In the room there were other men and parents. Some were Caucasian and some were from overseas. Ned was the only foreigner with a white girl friend. It did not bother him anymore than it did before. He had been through it. After four hours of waiting, Kay came out to fetch

Ned. "It is all done. They sucked it out. There are papers we have to sign", said Kay happily. They went in and looked at the papers and signed them. Kay went to get changed. The nurse who looked after Kay throughout the procedure was Indian. She came to Ned and introduced herself. "I am Nina. Kay really loves you. She thinks the world of you", said Nina. "Thank you. It's very kind of you. How was the pregnancy?", asked Ned. "The pregnancy was healthy. If she came a week later her belly would have shown distinctively", replied Nina. "Thank you", replied Ned. He was glad to know that it was a healthy pregnancy and sad as well. He did not want to know anymore. The nurse went to the office and handed Ned a packet. "What is it?", asked Ned. "Contraceptive. It is included in the bill", replied Nina and she handed Ned a bill of £500.00. By that time Kay came and paid with her credit card. They then left and went to the hotel. It was a four star hotel. Kay was a bit uncomfortable but did not complain at all as she felt free, with no worries and no uncertainty and no more stress and no more surprises. They stayed in the hotel for three nights. They went out to dinner every night and rested and visited few places. Ned settled the hotel bill and they were back. He dropped Kay at her home and drove back to London. From that day onwards they spoke almost everyday. Kay called mostly as she appreciated that Ned saw her through it. When Kay was settled and felt all right the calls went from everyday to twice a week as before. They continued seeing one another for short breaks. Then after few months the calls dropped down to once a months and meeting was once in three months. Then one day Kay called and tried to convince Ned that it would be better to be just friends as she did not want him to wait and waste his time. Ned was not bothered about the time for as long as it was okay with her but as Kay was trying hard and her best to be friends he agreed just to see what happens. "Okay. I do not mind as we both have busy schedule. If you really want to, then okay. But can I still have sex as a friend when I see you?", asked Ned jokingly. "Sure. But not if you have a girlfriend", replied Kay. "Well. I thought you want to cool it down because of time and schedule", said Ned. "I still want you to live your life in full. You are a good man and you will make a damn good husband?", said Kay. "Yeah… yeah… how about good husband to you?", joked Ned. "Stop it, will you?", replied Kay. "Well. I love you and always will. I wish you all the best. Keep in touch and perhaps we can go for a short break when you have time", said Ned. "We certainly will", replied Kay. Ned felt heavy. He did not know what to think. He had done what Kay wanted him to do for along time, to split up. They agreed to keep in touch but one week went there was nothing. Ned made several calls and left messages on messages with her parents. The second week, the same story. Then he received a letter on the third week.

"Dear Ned,
I hope you are keeping well and I miss you. You are my best friend and I hope I am yours too. I want to let you know that I am getting married next week to Andrew, a refined man like you whom I met at work. I hope you will understand.
Love Kay."

Ned read the very short letter. He was numb. He did not know what to think. It took a long time from knowing to getting engaged to getting married. He dropped himself in bed with the letter in his hand. But then he thought "Well, I am sure your parents are ecstatic seeing you walking on the aisle".

29

The next day Ned went to visit Shah who was pleased to see him. Ned was different. He got out of the car and said "come on man, get out of your room. There is much to live. Let's hit the hut …!!!", with dance music blaring in the car. From that day Ned was known as the three W's of the society, 'Women, Wine and Wealth'. He had it and flaunted it. He had a successful carrier, drove expensive car, had different girl every week and lived it…. Never looked back.

ISBN 141202012-3